Wait for Me
Phantom Horse

CHRISTINE PULLEIN-THOMPSON

illustrated by
Eric Rowe

AWARD PUBLICATIONS LIMITED

ISBN 0-86163-845-X

Text copyright © Christine Pullein-Thompson 1985
Illustrations copyright © Award Publications Limited 1997

This edition first published 1997 by
Award Publications Limited,
27 Longford Street, London NW1 3DZ

Printed in Italy

1

"She's all alone much of the time, poor kid. It's no life for a girl," said our help, Mrs Parkin. She was talking about the new family who had bought Hill Farm House, which had once been decrepit and tumbledown but was now done up with coaching lights at the end of the drive.

"What about her parents?" Mum asked.

"They're kind enough. I'm not complaining," replied Mrs Parkin with a sniff. "They fetch me, take me back, pay on the dot – over the odds often as not. It's just the kid's so much on her own, it isn't natural."

Mrs Parkin has worked for us for years. She always knows what is going on in the village.

"Why don't you ride over and call on her, Jean? Phantom needs exercise," suggested Mum.

"And what would I say – Are you lonely?"

"No, just stop and wave over the fence."

"They've got a swimming-pool, Jean. You and Angus could swim there sometimes, that would be nice, wouldn't it?" said Mrs Parkin.

"Will you ride over with me, Angus?" I asked my brother, who was looking out of the window.

"If you insist," he said, turning to face me. "After all we might like her, and they must have pots of money to buy a place like that."

"She's called Rachel," said Mrs Parkin, before switching on the vacuum cleaner and drowning all further conversation.

It was summer, with the orchard full of buttercups and the apples beginning to change colour on the trees. There were dancing clouds in the sky and a smell of roses in the garden. Our horses were standing together in the paddock under the oak-tree, which is nearly as old as the cottage where we live.

"I bet she's awful," said Angus, grooming grey Killarney.

"She'll talk as though she has a marble in her mouth," I suggested.

"No, a plum," replied Angus, laughing. "A large purple one."

"The house is ruined anyway," I said. "It doesn't look like a farmhouse any more."

"It looks American – an American ranch house," said my brother, fetching his saddle and bridle from the tack room.

Phantom's coat was gleaming gold, his mane silver, his muscles rippling beneath his skin. I had never seen him look fitter.

He opened his mouth for the bit and stood patiently to be saddled. Another minute and we were riding away down the tree-shaded road, the clip-clop of hoofs like poetry in my ears.

"Rachel what?" asked Angus.

"I don't know."

"It's going to be a scorcher today," observed Angus a minute later. "Hotter than yesterday, and I could sure do with a swim."

"Is that why you came?"

"I guess so."

"Stop being American."

"I'm practising. I'm going to pretend I'm from the States," said Angus.

Hill Farm House is a mile from us. It stands at the end of a short drive, which a year ago had been a rutted track with nettles on each side. The house then had hidden behind a tangle of ivy, brambles and overgrown roses. The windows had been grimy, and dogs had guarded the shabby back door. Now all was changed. The dogs and the creepers had gone. The bricks were revealed, the windows restored and cleaned. The huge, battered farm buildings, which had stood on both sides of the house, had been demolished and replaced by grass and shrubs. A grey wood smoke no longer emerged from the chimneys, hens no longer scratched busily in the yard. Two garages had replaced the cowsheds at the back, and the paddock, once fenced by overgrown hedges, was now enclosed by a white-railed fence, the ancient horse pond becoming a feature of the garden with a fountain worked by electricity. Once it had looked like a Domesday house, now it looked like a rich man's folly. The sight brought tears to my eyes. "I hate looking at it. I keep thinking of all the horses which must have drunk at the old pond, and the barns were so lovely," I said.

There was a notice which read CAUTION – GUARD DOGS. I pointed at it while Angus said, "You can't stop change. I'll hold Phantom while you knock on the door. There aren't any dogs because there's no sound of barking."

"Oh yeah? Why me?" I asked.

"Because you're more tactful."

"Flattery won't get you anywhere," I said, dismounting nevertheless, wondering what to say as I handed Angus my reins.

There were steps up to the front door. Once you had to thump on the door with your fists, willing the dogs not to bite. Now there was a new bell which I pushed and pushed again.

"Obviously she isn't in," I said, with relief in my voice.

"So we can go home; it's time for elevenses and I feel like bread and cheese," said Angus, who was always hungry and couldn't last from one meal to the next.

"Hang on, I hear footsteps," I said.

Another second and Rachel appeared – at least we guessed it was Rachel. She had long tawny hair, varnished nails and was wearing a bikini. She had eyes which were not English – Slavic I guessed – and long brown legs. Her feet were bare. Angus gave a small gasp and then, squaring his shoulders, announced, "I'm Angus and this is my sister Jean. We live in Sparrow Cottage and thought we would see whether you are all right."

"All right? Of course I'm all right. I was by the swimming-pool getting a tan. Are these your horses?"

I nodded. "Phantom and Killarney. Phantom's American, Killarney's Irish and we're English-Scottish," I told her.

Rachel stood staring at Angus before saying, "Mrs Parkin thought we should meet. You have her two mornings a week, is that right?"

"Yes, we have for years and years," I replied quickly.

"And your father works for the government, and it's very hush-hush," she continued.

"Yes, but it's not always hush-hush," replied Angus, laughing so that I thought: He likes her, he's smitten.

"Sometimes it's quite ordinary, sometimes he works from home, and sometimes he is sent places," I explained.

There was a huge dish-like gadget by the house. "It's something to do with satellites," whispered Angus.

"My father is in communications," explained Rachel. "That's why we've got a burglar alarm and that silly notice about guard dogs. He has masses of very complicated equipment. There's more inside. Do you like swimming?"

"Yes, very much," replied Angus quickly.

"You must come and swim then," she said. "Come this afternoon, and by the way, I love horses. I'm going to buy one. Will you help me choose?"

"Of course," replied Angus.

"You see I don't know anything about them. I've only ridden at a riding-school, but I would like an Anglo-Arab," continued Rachel.

"We'll help you any time," offered Angus. "Just name the day."

"Mrs Parkin suggested Reading market," Rachel said. "That's on a Friday, isn't it?"

"But quite unsuitable," I told her.

"We needn't buy anything. We can just go and look," said my brother. "Just to get your eye in. There won't be Anglo-Arabs, but you might just find a bargain."

"Father has given me a thousand pounds," she said. "Is that enough?"

"Hardly, but we might be lucky," Angus replied, beaming at her, showing off his even teeth, his brown eyes full of appreciation, while I felt like an intruder, an outsider of no significance whatsoever.

"We had better go home, or you won't get your elevenses, Angus," I said, mounting Phantom again.

"Friday then," Angus said.

He looked at Rachel who asked, "But how do we get there?"

"My mother will take us," Angus replied, without looking at me.

"Wear dark glasses and bring a large hand-kerchief," I shouted over my shoulder, riding away.

"Jean always cries at the market. She doesn't like horses going for meat," explained my brother, before catching up with me.

"What's the hurry?" Rachel called. "Come and swim whenever you like. Don't forget."

"Wow!" exclaimed Angus when we were out of earshot. "She's like a film star, isn't she?"

"You don't like swimming, you always say you don't, anyway," I answered.

"Depends whom I'm swimming with," replied Angus, laughing.

"She looks older than us," I said as we reached the road.

"Only more sophisticated," Angus said happily, which made me think: He's seventeen, soon he will be leaving home. Soon he will be grown up and the best years will have gone. I did not want to grow up. I wanted life to go on being just the same, with hunter trials and Pony Club camp. I did not want to earn money or have a career. Dad thought I should take a secretarial course, Mum wanted me to learn about computers, while I just wanted life to stand still.

We put the horses in our old-fashioned stables because of the flies. The sun was still shining and Mrs Parkin was drinking tea with Mum in the kitchen.

"She's asked us to go swimming," Angus said, taking off his riding-hat. "She made Jean look like a country cousin."

I looked at Angus and said nothing. Once we had been close, now we were growing apart; it was a fact of life, nothing would change it.

"Did you like her, Jean?" Mum asked.

"She's all right," I said. "But she wasn't interested in me, only in Angus."

"She wants us to help her find a horse. Can you take us to Reading market on Friday? The sale will be on the first Friday in August, won't it?" asked Angus.

"That's right. Is today Monday?" asked Mum.

"Yes," said Mrs Parkin. "Well, I must get on. Anyone seen my dusters?"

I remembered I had borrowed them to polish Phantom's bit and went out to the tack room. It was very hot now and everything seemed dry and still, except for the flies which were everywhere. I kept remembering Hill Farm House as it had once been, reeking of history.

Angus was still talking about Rachel when I returned to the kitchen. He was saying, "Honestly, she looks just like a film star. She's stunning; that's the word, stunning."

"So, Jean, you didn't like her?" insisted Mum, taking the dusters from me.

"She's not my sort of person," I said. "She

looks quite a lot older than me."

"Mrs Parkin says she's only sixteen. I'll just write Reading market in my diary or I'll forget," Mum said.

Angus returned to Hill Farm House in the afternoon, while I spent the afternoon schooling Phantom. It was very hot.

"Why didn't you go with Angus? You are a goat," said Mum, when I went inside to drink three glasses of orange squash.

"They don't need me," I said. "Can't you see Angus has fallen in love?"

"Well, it had to happen sometime. At least she's close to home!" replied Mum, laughing.

Angus returned at eight o'clock. "I've met her parents. They're super. They gave me a Campari and orange. I could have had anything I liked. They wanted me to stay to dinner," he said. "They're not like us at all. They may be getting three horses, one for each of them – so we had better start looking straight away. And, oh, they want to meet you Mum, and Dad. They are terrifically hospitable, real live wires. Rachel's mother is beautiful, too. Her father looks a man of the world. He speaks three languages and drives a Mercedes. They made me feel a bit of a pauper, actually."

"Some of us don't wear our wealth on our sleeve," replied Mum.

"Everything's new; from Harrods actually.

They used to live abroad. They'll certainly wake up this sleepy old village," continued Angus.

"Where are they going to put their horses? They've knocked down the old stables," I said.

"They're going to build new ones."

"They'll need a groom," I said. "I can't see Rachel mucking out."

"Perhaps you would like the job," suggested Angus, laughing.

I threw some orange squash at him and could hear him still laughing as I wandered outside, wondering why people have to grow up and fall in love.

The summer is ruined, I thought. I wish Rachel and her parents had never moved here. I saw Angus talking of nothing else, morning, noon and night.

I saw him riding with Rachel through the woods I loved. I saw him talking like she did, thinking like she did, becoming a different person. For years we had done everything together. Now I would have to go it alone.

2

On Friday, Rachel arrived at our place at ten minutes to nine. Dad had left for work and the kitchen was piled high with washing-up. The horses were waiting to be brought in.

Angus opened the door to her still in his pyjamas, his hair in chaos and his feet bare.

"You're early. I thought we were picking you up," he cried, his face slowly turning to the colour of beetroot.

"I thought I would see where you lived. It's such a lovely morning." She was wearing jeans, the expensive kind with the right label on the back, an open necked shirt and high-heeled, thin-strapped sandals.

"Come in. It is Rachel, isn't it?" asked Mum. "Angus, go and get dressed."

"Yes, Rachel Finbow," she said. "What a quaint old place."

I fled to the stables. Phantom was standing at the gate nickering. The sun was merciless in its heat, the sky cloudless, the grass turning yellow.

She isn't real I thought, as I brought the horses in. She's like a dummy in a shop window. She's pretending, wearing a veneer. Angus is so smitten he can't see it, but I can feel it in my bones.

When I returned indoors, Mum was showing Rachel over the cottage. I wondered what she thought of my bedroom, full of china horses, my teddy bear on my bed, my bookshelves stacked with childish books as well as Dickens, Jane Austen and *Wuthering Heights*. Piles of *Riding* in one corner. Photographs of Phantom everywhere. No make-up to be seen.

Later we drank coffee in the kitchen and Rachel talked to Mum. Then Angus appeared, full of apologies.

"We don't need to be there until eleven because they sell the tack first," Mum said. "Unless you want to shop."

We did not want to shop, so Angus and Rachel talked. Then they sat in the sitting-room listening to Dad's records and looking into each other's eyes. Soon they'll be holding hands, I thought.

Rachel wanted to ride. "Couldn't I ride Jean's horse?" she asked Angus. "Then we can go out together."

Angus looked at me.

"Sorry, you can't. He's peculiar," I answered. "Nobody could ride him when we caught him in Virginia. I'm the only person he trusts."

She doesn't believe me, I thought, and imagined her on Phantom, his eyes fearful, her legs too far back, her hands moving up and down as she trotted.

"Then I could ride your horse, Angus," she suggested.

"But I can't ride Phantom," Angus said.

Suddenly it was time to go. I put on my dark glasses and filled the pockets of my jeans with tissues. We walked straight out of the cottage as we always did. I remember the brick path was strewn with rose petals and somewhere a bird was singing. The horses were dozing in the stable, sleek in their summer coats.

Mum was wearing a denim skirt, a checked shirt, flat shoes. She looked young, too young to be Angus's mother.

The road to Reading was full of cars. Everyone seemed to be going shopping.

"Do you like it here, Rachel?" Mum asked.

"Yes, it's terrific."

"It's very nice of you to ask us round to drinks on Sunday."

"It's a pleasure," Rachel said. "I'm so glad your husband can come. My parents very much want to meet him."

I thought of Dad, tall, his hair turning grey. Lately he had seemed withdrawn, hardly with us. Mum had said, "He has worries. But he

19

can't talk about them; that's what makes it so hard."

"He's rather busy at the moment," she said to Rachel, stopping at traffic-lights. "I hope he can make it. He brings a lot of work home, you know."

"That's the penalty of success," said Rachel, sounding at least twenty years old.

The market was full of farmers in caps and boots in spite of the heat, small children holding their parents' hands, and horsy women talking about hocks and knees, about necks and heads, about throughpins and splints. Foals shrieked for their dams and horses' eyes searched about anxiously for lost friends. Two-year-olds were shod and advertised as "Quiet to ride", while old horses stood resting tired legs, awaiting their end. A thoroughbred was crib-biting, while a bay pony dug frantically at the concrete with his hoofs. I was glad of my dark glasses because my eyes were full of tears.

Angus led Rachel by the arm, reading out aloud from the catalogue, pointing out defects in a knowledgeable manner, saying, "That one isn't big enough; and that one says nothing about being quiet to ride so he could be a rogue."

Rachel rushed straight to the chestnuts and greys. She wanted four white socks and a blaze, or a grey with an araby head and a ewe neck.

"There's nothing here, can't you see?" I

said to them, swallowing my tears.

"Do shut up. We're enjoying ourselves, aren't we, Rachel?" Angus said.

She nodded, staring at a black without a speck of white anywhere, asking, "What about this one, Angus?"

"He's sixteen-two. You would need a box to mount him," Angus said.

"He would do for my father."

"But we're not buying for your father today."

We bought ourselves coffee in thick mugs, and fattening lardy-cake. The noise was deafening. "It's like a slave market," I said.

"You're too emotional," replied Angus, "and I bet you're crying behind those idiotic glasses."

I did not answer, for now I was imagining Phantom for sale with the other horses, having his mouth wrenched open, his teeth examined, his legs felt, his eyes looked into without a word of kindness from anyone.

"They're fetching good prices," said Angus, trying to sound knowledgeable. "They'll be cheaper in the autumn."

By now it was noon. We went outside and found Mum sitting in our rather battered estate car. "Hurry," she shouted. "I'm roasting to death."

"Why didn't you tell us? You should have come inside," Angus said.

"Because I'm like Jean – it makes me cry,"

Mum said, starting the engine.

Rachel made us stop so that she could buy ice creams. "I know I'm delaying things, but I shall be all alone once I'm home," she said. "And this is my contribution to the petrol."

"Are your parents always away then?" asked Mum.

"Not always, but mostly." She had a way of smiling sweetly. I can't describe it in any other way, and yet it seemed false just the same.

Soon we were stuck in a traffic jam. "Have you no radio? No cassettes?" asked Rachel, obviously amazed.

"No, not at the moment," Mum replied.

At last we left the main road. Soon we could see the church, the pub, the village shop, then the road narrowed, and tucked away in a valley lay Sparrow Cottage.

"Can you drop me first, please?" asked Rachel. "I've suddenly remembered that Mother was to phone me at one o'clock and it is important."

So we flew past Sparrow Cottage and a few minutes later drew up outside Hill Farm House with a screech of brakes. Another satellite dish had been added alongside the one already there and stood stark and alien against the summer sky.

"I can't thank you enough," said Rachel, getting out.

"I can't wait to see your paddock full of horses," replied Angus, politely.

"Come and swim any time. You, too," Rachel told Mum, running towards the house, "and your husband."

"See you Sunday," shouted Mum.

"All of you," Rachel insisted, waving farewell.

"What do you think of her?" Angus asked as Mum turned the car.

"I don't know. I honestly don't. I have my reservations –"

"Why?" asked Angus, sounding disappointed.

"I don't know. She seems to be trying too hard," Mum said.

"But there's nothing wrong with that," Angus retorted. "Personally, I find her manners perfect."

"I wish the weather would change. I want to jump and the ground's like a rock," I said suddenly, sick of discussing Rachel Finbow.

I find it hard to describe the next few moments. Mum told Angus to carry the shopping. The petals were still on the brick path. The sun was still shining. Nothing seemed changed, except that the back door was open.

"How extraordinary! I'm sure I closed it," exclaimed Mum. "It's lucky your father isn't here, he would be furious. Who was last out anyway?"

"Not me," said Angus.

"I can't remember," I said.

We went inside. "Funny, it smells of tobacco and none of us smoke . . . Put the shopping on the table, Angus, please," Mum said, her voice suddenly shrill with anxiety.

She hurried out of the kitchen and we heard her gasp, before she came back running and shrieking, "We've been burgled. Come and look. They have been into all the drawers, upstairs and downstairs. The whole place is in chaos, just look. Oh my God . . ."

All the cupboards were open; the drawers pulled out, chairs toppled over, clothes and

papers everywhere. Mum kept saying, "Oh my God, my God," which made everything seem worse.

Angus tried to console her by saying, "Don't worry, Mum, they haven't taken anything. There was nothing valuable to take; you left your jewellery in the bank last month, don't you remember, Mum? Don't cry. I'll tidy it up."

I suddenly thought: Phantom! The tack! Supposing the horses have gone? I rushed out of the cottage, shouting, "What about the horses?"

But they were all right, standing with their backs to the doors, resting their hind legs, and the tack was safe, too.

Mum was on the phone talking to Dad when I returned to the house. I could hear his voice shouting from the other end of the line, "Didn't you lock up? Haven't I told you time and time again to lock up?"

"Tell him they would have got in through the windows," said Angus, "or through the other door."

But I knew he was wrong because the windows at Sparrow Cottage are old and tiny, and the front door has three bolts and a chain on it.

"But it was morning and we were only gone two hours," Mum said. "Who expects burglars in the morning?"

"Have you rung the police?" asked Dad, changing tack.

"Not yet."

"Well, get on to them at once. I'll try to get back as soon as I can. Don't touch anything," shouted Dad, banging down the receiver.

"He sounds in a right old flap," commented Angus, tidying up.

"Leave it alone. Don't touch anything," shouted Mum. "Leave it, Angus. Do you hear?"

"It's all right, I'm not a dog."

"There's no need to be cheeky."

"The horses are all right," I said.

"Oh, why did it happen?" wept Mum, while Angus stood dialling 999. The whole day was spoilt, and the time we spent at the market seemed to belong to another world.

"They'll be over as soon as they can," said Angus, replacing the receiver. "If we're not having any lunch, and you don't want me to clear up, I think I'll pop over to Hill Farm House. At least I'll get a welcome there."

"You can't just buzz off as though nothing has happened. You've got to stay, the police may want to see you," Mum said.

"I'll make an omelette," I offered. "And there's some cake in the tin."

But Mum didn't feel like eating, so I went outside and, putting my arms round Phantom, told him what had happened. Presently there was a crunch of tyres on the gravel and the police arrived.

Later I found that my room had been visited too. My clothes were strewn everywhere, my nicest china horse was smashed and someone had scrawled some terrible words above my bed, words I could not understand, but which Dad was later to describe as those of the cesspit.

3

Dad looked haggard when he arrived.

"It's all right, there's nothing valuable missing, only a few odds and ends like my camera and Angus's cassette-recorder, and we can claim for them on the insurance, darling," said Mum, flapping like a hen as she followed him from room to room.

"Have they fingerprinted? Have the police fingerprinted?" shouted Dad, as though we were all deaf. "Where's Angus?"

"At Hill Farm House," Mum answered.

"He's in love with Rachel," I added.

"We'll soon get everything tidy. We're not the first people to be burgled," Mum said.

But Dad was like someone demented, going from room to room with sweat running off his face, muttering curses under his breath, asking, "Why do you both keep following me around?"

"Go out, go out on Phantom, Jean. Leave him to me," Mum said.

So I tacked up Phantom and rode through

the valley where the corn was being cut. I thought that Dad was going mad and none of us knew why, not even Mum. If I ever marry, I'll marry a farmer, I thought. Then I can always be at home and so can he, and we'll have loads of horses and it won't matter about the price of oats or the price of hay because we'll grow them; we'll spend our lives in old clothes and be happy and never have to know people like Rachel Finbow.

Phantom was lively and, as the flies retreated in the gathering dusk, midges appeared in clouds to drive us frantic. When I returned home, Angus was there, singing as he mucked out Killarney's box.

"You should have come to Hill Farm House. We had the most fantastic tea – Black Forest gateau, ice cream, chocolate biscuits," he said, "and as for music, well there's just about everything on CD."

"What about the cottage? Is it cleared up yet?" I asked.

"Not yet. They're in a mood," Angus told me. "Not speaking, actually. Dad's drinking whisky."

"Poor them," I said.

"Poor me. I've lost my cassette-recorder and I'm not grumbling, am I? Not a whimper," said Angus.

I untacked Phantom and turned him out.

"By the way, we're seeing Maureen Nunn tomorrow about horses," Angus told me, emptying the wheelbarrow. Maureen Nunn is our local horse dealer.

"How are we getting there? You're not asking Mum again, are you?" I asked.

"No, not this time. Rachel's mum is taking us in the Mercedes," Angus said. "Okay? Or is that wrong too?"

"No, but you don't need me," I answered, hanging up Phantom's headcollar. "You can manage. You know more than I do."

"No, I don't. Anyway, two heads are better than one. Maureen likes you, she won't cheat you."

"She won't cheat anyone," I said.

"You can't refuse."

I like Maureen. I like her yard. I like looking at her horses. The chance to ride some of them was a chance I couldn't bear to turn down. "All right. What time?" I asked.

"Ten o'clock at the front gate."

"Have you told Maureen we're coming?"

"Yes, and she's got several animals which might do. You want to come, don't you? You don't mind?"

I shook my head and I think we both dreaded going indoors, but it was after eight o'clock now and long past suppertime.

"What on earth is the matter with Dad?" I

asked, following Angus into the house.

"He's lost something – and it's hush-hush," Angus replied.

By ten o'clock next day the cottage was ship-shape again and the weather was scorching. The fields shimmered beneath the sun, the flowers wilted. The cottage windows were open. Mrs Parkin stood shaking mats while Dad was sitting in a deckchair sorting through papers, an ancient panama hat on his greying head.

"Don't be late back, there's something special for lunch," Mum told us, still looking anxious, her neat brow a mass of furrows.

"Can we ask Rachel and her mother to lunch?" asked Angus.

Mum shook her head.

"You're so inhospitable," Angus complained, while I thought that it was typical of the Finbows to be late. They are those sort of people, I thought. All manners on the surface, but underneath they only care for themselves.

"Here they are," cried Angus.

The Mercedes looked too big for our lane. Rachel's mother pushed a button and the window on her side disappeared into the door.

"Hop in," she said. "You get in the front, Jean; it is Jean, isn't it?"

She was like Rachel, only the colour of her auburn hair wasn't real and her clothes were even more expensive than Rachel's. She smelled marvellous.

"This *is* exciting, isn't it? I've never looked at a horse before," she told me, driving on.

Rachel leaned over to push a cassette into the player. The tune was the one Angus played over and over in his room upstairs.

"Which way?" Rachel's mother called above the music.

"Left, then right, Mrs Finbow," I said.

"I'm not Mrs Finbow; the name is Winter, Melanie Winter," she told me. "What a fantastic day, we could be in the South of France."

"Now right," I said a moment later. "Slow down, we're almost there." Suddenly I wished we had come without Rachel and her mother. I felt ashamed of their rich appearance; they were simply not our sort of people. Hearing the car, Maureen appeared from the house. She is small with a mass of curly hair, a smile which shows a row of large, uneven teeth, and her eyes are grey. She was wearing jeans and a bright red shirt with a wide belt round her midriff. "This way," she said. "I have three lined up for you. You can ride them for me, can't you, Jean?"

I nodded. Once she had asked me to work for her part-time, just in the holidays, but my parents had said no. "You'll break your neck or your teeth," Mum had said. Dad said I'd become even more horsy than I was already.

A boy wearing wellington boots led out a piebald and stood him up for us.

"No thank you. He's a gipsy horse," said Mrs Winter. "My husband likes style. Whatever we buy must have style."

"Manners matter more than style," I told her. "Not to mention soundness."

The piebald was put away and a sturdy bay led out. "No, too plain," said Mrs Winter. "Out of the question. David would never stand for him."

She's buying a dress, I thought, not a horse. She doesn't know the first thing about them. She doesn't care about Rachel. She only cares about status.

Maureen sighed and looked over to Rachel. "I have a part-bred Arab, but can you ride it? That's the question, isn't it?" she asked.

"I can learn," Rachel said.

"But it takes time."

"We'll pay for her to have lessons," said Mrs Winter. "Let us see the Arab one, it sounds more likely." I looked at Angus. He was looking at the ground.

The boy brought out the part-bred Arab. More than fifteen hands, she was chestnut with three white socks, a wide forehead and cheek, and an eye which was both large and spirited.

"Ah, now we may do business," said Mrs Winter.

I suppose it was inevitable that we should buy the chestnut. I rode her and I must say she went superbly. She felt as though she had springs in her pasterns and could go for ever without growing tired.

"She's lovely, but she's not a beginner's horse," I said, drawing rein, the sun burning through my shirt.

"But Rachel will learn. We can have her taught," insisted Mrs Winter.

"I am not too happy about it, but if Jean will help . . .?" Maureen began.

"Yes of course we'll help," said Angus in a loud voice, answering for both of us. I was too much of a fool to argue, too polite, too undecided. Yet I doubted whether Rachel would ever manage the chestnut, which was called Marli, though probably she had a more complicated and far longer name on her papers, and I presumed she had papers.

Mrs Winter was pleased. "She will look good in the paddock. She will complement the garden," she said, as though she were buying a statue rather than a horse.

Rachel all the while, said nothing, just stood languidly staring into space. This surprised me so that I turned to her asking, "What do you think? Do you think you will ever manage her?"

She started before returning to reality with a jerk. "Yes, in time," she said vaguely. "In time, everything takes time . . ."

We walked into the house and stood in a large, old-fashioned dining-room, with cheap rugs on old brown linoleum and antimacassars on chairs. It smelled empty and unused.

"Are you really sure? Wouldn't you like to look at a few more horses, Mrs Winter?" I asked. "There's no hurry."

"Yes, of course . . . but I know what I like," she said, taking a cheque-book out of her beautiful leather handbag, followed by a gold pen.

"But Rachel didn't try her," I insisted.

"Rachel will learn."

She wrote the cheque in flowery handwriting and, saying, "David will be pleased," she handed it to Maureen with a smile.

"You'll have to ride with Jean and Angus," Maureen told Rachel. "Do what they say. Don't go out on your own to start with."

The cheque was for three thousand pounds and Maureen folded it in two before putting it in a drawer.

"What about a vet? We haven't had her vetted," I said.

"I'll write out a warranty for you, Mrs Winter. You don't want to wait for a vet, do you?"

"Not if I can have a warranty," said Mrs Winter.

"It will save you a lot of money."

"What about tack?" I asked.

"I can supply that, too," said Maureen.

We returned to the yard. The boy brought out an array of saddles. "Have a general purpose one," my brother said. I had become speechless. Life seemed suddenly out of control and I could see nothing but disaster ahead. If Rachel is killed in a riding accident, it will be our fault, I thought, because we brought her here . . .

Mrs Winter had chosen a saddle; it was brand new and black. "Now for a bridle," she said.

Angus helped them to choose. He was not looking at me any more. I am sure he knew how I felt. We tried the tack on Marli. It fitted.

"Right, there we are. We needn't go in. I will write the cheque on the bonnet of my car," insisted Mrs Winter. I could not help recalling my parents arguing over every pound and here was Mrs Winter spending far more than three thousand pounds without a flutter of her eyelids.

"You see how rich they are," Angus muttered to me. "Stop staring. A thousand pounds to them is like a hundred pounds to us."

"But they shouldn't be spending so much. They don't need to and everything is unsuitable," I said. "It's a tragedy . . ."

Maureen was looking pleased now. She smiled at me and Angus, and I knew the smile was her way of saying, "Thank you for bringing me such excellent business." Then I heard her saying, "Jean will ride the mare over to your place, won't you, Jean?" I heard myself saying, "Yes," though my whole being cried: No. No, never. She is unsuitable . . . It's all a terrible mistake.

"She'll have to live by herself. You realise that," I told Maureen when the others had gone.

"She'll get used to it."

"The field is fenced with rails; there's no shade," I continued. "What are we going to do?"

"Stop worrying. Greg, tack up the mare, will you?" Maureen told the boy.

I looked at Greg properly for the first time. He was doing the job I might have done. He had dark curly hair, blue eyes and a mouth which looked too serious for his age, which couldn't have been more than seventeen.

"You know the way, don't you?"

"Yes, of course. Is she traffic-proof?" I asked.

"Not bad . . ." I wondered what that meant!

Greg held my stirrup while I mounted. I sat down gingerly on the new saddle before tightening the new white nylon girth.

"All right?" he asked. I nodded. Marli danced out of the drive, went sideways down the road, her head high, her neck arched. She was beautifully schooled and went like a dream.

I turned into the woods and suddenly the blistering heat was gone; the ground was a lace-work of shadows cast by the branches of trees overhead. Long-fallen leaves gave it a softness.

A rabbit fled at our approach. So tall and ancient were the trees that, for a moment, I felt as
though I was riding through a cathedral. There
was no sound now besides that of Marli's hoofs
gently landing on soft earth and the creak of
saddle and the jingle of bit. Yet in spite of a
feeling of intense happiness, I was also pos-
sessed by a feeling of impending doom. Why
did we get involved? I wondered. Once involved, why did we let the Winters buy such a
horse? Plus why was Rachel a Finbow and not
a Winter? Where was her real father?

I touched Marli with my legs and she trotted,
a wonderful balanced trot, and I wondered why
we had not forced Rachel to try the mare. Why
had we been so insipid and so feeble that now I
was saddled with teaching Rachel to ride when
I wanted to school Phantom and get ready for
Pony Club camp? Also to read *Mansfield Park*
and Chaucer so that I would be able to pass
fast-approaching exams. I saw myself standing
in the beautifully railed paddock at Hill Farm
House trying to get Rachel to sit still on her
beautiful saddle; to keep her hands still, to be
gentle and firm at the same time. It would take
weeks, not days. Now we were out of the
woods in the valley which I love more than
anywhere else on earth, and the distant corn
shimmered in the heat like a gently-moving sea,
and the sun was so hot that it burned like a

furnace on my back, and the track was hard and dusty, and the distant main road cluttered with cars moving tail to tail towards a faraway coast.

I love every inch of this valley and wherever I go the vision of it is with me, buried in the back of my mind. It isn't really my valley but in my mind it will always be the valley which leads to home.

Dominic, who is a friend of ours, was loading straw into the back of a trailer and turned to wave and call, "Where's Phantom? Is that a new horse?"

So I stopped and told him about the new people at Hill Farm House. But he knew no more than I did.

"They're very well off, but no one knows where they made their money. My mother says 'easy come, easy go.' They shouldn't be in the country, not really," he said. "And what do they want a mare like this one for?" he asked, patting Marli. "They haven't got a stable and only the one paddock. Can the girl ride?"

I shook my head. "Not much. I'm supposed to be teaching her," I confessed.

"Rather you than me," said Dominic. "By the way, would Angus like to turn an honest penny? We need some help."

"Yes, of course. But what about me?"

"You, too. But it sounds as though you've

got your hands full. Mind you charge them for lessons, they can pay," said Dominic, turning back to the straw.

"I'll tell Angus anyway," I said.

"Yes. He can start tomorrow if he likes, after milking, say nine o'clock," Dominic said, his hair bleached by the sun, broad shouldered, his feet firm on the acres which one day he would inherit. "Come this way again, Jean. We haven't seen you for a long time," he said, turning to smile at me. "We miss you, Jean, and you know you're always welcome."

"Thank you, I will." Marli was eager to be off. We trotted on between the fields, reached the road, climbed right up the long hill to Hill Farm House. I thought of my relationship with Dominic, which is one-sided, since he cares for me intensely and I only want a platonic friendship. The trouble is there's nothing to discover in Dominic, I thought. It's all there on his face – honesty, hard work, devotion. But half an hour alone with him and I am bored to the marrow of my bones.

Marli shied at the traffic, then leaped out in front of a bus. I put out my arm, then pushed Marli into a spanking trot. I could see Hill Farm House in the distance with cars parked outside and men working close to the house erecting a tangle of wires and masts, something which was beyond my grasp.

I reached the yard and drew rein. There was
no one waiting for me, no one looking out of a
window, only the sound of laughter coming
from the swimming-pool.

Looking at me, a man in dungarees called,

"They're swimming, love. Go round the side of the house; tie the horse up." But not by the reins I thought, standing undecided, Marli's neck lathered with sweat.

Finally I opened the paddock gate, took off her tack and let her go. She stood neighing for her friends while I looked in vain for a trough of water. I felt very low in spirit now. Marli will be so lonely, I thought. Who will look after her? There's no shade anywhere.

Then I walked round the side of the house and found a crowd of people with cut crystal glasses in their hands. "Why, it's Jean," cried Mrs Winter. "Come and have a drink."

Angus was there too, in red swimming trunks. "This is my little sister," he said with a silly smirk.

"There's no water for Marli," I said, embarrassed as I stood there smelling of horse in my faded jodhpurs, cotton shirt and brown boots.

"We'll see to that presently," said a tall man, detaching himself from the others. "I'm David Winter."

He was heavily bearded; his eyes were small and brown, his nose fleshy, his lips full and red, his teeth small by comparison. He was broad shouldered, hairy chested, and was wearing nothing but white swimming trunks held up by a red belt, overlapped by an enormous stomach.

He shook me by the hand. "Nice to meet

you, Jean. Did the mare come over all right?"
he asked.

"Yes, but she needs water," I said.

"Water, yes, water. Rachel, water for your
mare," he called.

Rachel took me to the kitchen, which was
immaculate. She was dressed in a bikini and
bare footed. We found a plastic washing-up
bowl and had to fill it three times before
Marli's thirst was quenched.

"You must get her a trough," I told Rachel.
"She'll need at least eight gallons a day in this
weather."

"I'll see to it later. I'll ask one of the work-
men. Are you coming back to the pool?" Rachel
asked.

"No thanks," I said, and started for home. I
noticed that there was now a brass sign on the
gatepost. It read: WINTER AND FINBOW, WORLD-
WIDE COMMUNICATIONS SERVICES LTD.

The workman in the dungarees called, "Did
you find them, love?"

"Yes, thanks," I shouted.

Marli was standing by the gate whinnying
piteously. Avoiding her eye I ran along the
drive, then on down the road, my head as
heavy as a wet bale of hay.

Mum was standing at our gate. "I was getting anxious," she said.

"I was delivering the mare. The Winters'

45

mare – they've bought something," I explained impatiently. "Angus is still there. They've bought an Arab mare."

"Why didn't they bring you home?"

"I don't think it even occurred to them," I answered, gulping down a glass of water in the kitchen.

"They could have rung me," Mum said. "Lunch is dried up."

"I don't think they have regular meals, just snacks round the swimming-pool," I said, and imagined Angus swallowing caviar, followed by smoked salmon sandwiches.

"I wish we weren't going on Sunday. They aren't our sort of people," Mum told me, placing a bowl of salad on the table. "But your father's really keen to meet them. I can't think why."

"He's too serious for them; they'll laugh at his striped shirt. They'll probably be in swimming trunks and bikinis. I think they live in them," I told her.

"We'd better pray for rain, then," Mum said.

"Actually, I'm very worried about Marli. She's very highly strung and quite unsuitable," I said.

"But I thought you went to advise them."

"We did, but somehow it went wrong. Now I've got to teach Rachel to ride. She's older than me and very sophisticated, and I'm terrified," I confessed, swallowing lettuce. "And I couldn't like them in a thousand years, Mum. Angus thinks they're marvellous, but I don't. I don't even like Rachel, in fact I hate her," I continued, "because she's everything I'm not. I would never choose her for a friend. She's like a model and she doesn't care one bit for Marli. That's what is so awful. None of them do. So why did they buy her?"

"As a status symbol. So that they can talk about Rachel's Arab mare to their friends in London," Mum told me. "They want to be more acceptable and to keep up with their rich friends. That's my guess anyway."

"David Winter wants to hunt; he wants a hunter," I said.

"For the same reason. He wants to sound smart, to look the part. He won't hunt, you can be sure of that."

Suddenly I did not want any more lunch. I stood by the window looking out, imagining Marli pacing the paddock. "It makes me want to cry," I said.

"I'm not surprised," replied Mum.

"Angus likes them," I continued, with a choke in my voice.

"But only for the moment and only because they treat him as someone special, as a grown-up. It's just a phase," Mum told me. But I did not believe her. I saw the whole summer ruined.

Angus no longer at home, Rachel dominating
every day.

Then I heard hoofbeats in the lane. Phantom
neighed, followed by Killarney. I opened the
kitchen door and dashed outside. Marli was in
the yard drenched with sweat. She was shaking
visibly and there was blood streaming from her
knee, slowly turning the white sock below
bright scarlet.

I fetched a headcollar and put it over her
shapely ears. Her breath was coming in gasps,
her sides heaved. "Shall I ring the vet?" asked
Mum.

"I think so. We don't know whether she's
had her tet, do we?" I said.

Then a car stopped with a screech of brakes
and David Winter, Rachel and Angus spilled
into the yard, still in their swimsuits.

"She jumped the fence, or tried to, and hit
the rail," shouted Angus. "Is she all right?"

"I don't know. She's bleeding pretty badly.
Mum's sending for the vet. Hang on to her
while I get Phantom out, she had better have
his box." Suddenly we were together again, on
the same side, understanding one another without the need of words, while David Winter and
Rachel Finbow looked on.

"He's on his way, they got hold of him on
his radio," Mum said, reappearing. "Does she
need a tourniquet?"

Angus was bending over the wound now, while Mum rushed for wadding and bandages to stop the bleeding and I held Marli, watching relief flood into her eyes.

"It's all right, you'll be all right here," I told her, while Killarney, looking over his door, nickered softly.

The two strangers were forgotten. They might just as well have been at home.

Then David Winter started to talk about our burglary. I suppose he had heard about it from Mrs Parkin, who knows everything that goes on in the village.

"It must have been a terrible shock for you," he said to Mum.

"It was. I'm still shaking," she said.

"Did they take much?"

"There wasn't too much to take," answered Mum wearily. "I keep my jewellery in the bank."

"It's happening all the time. It's worse in London. Why don't you go in for a burglar alarm?"

"I don't think we could manage one. We would keep setting it off by mistake. Here comes the vet," said Mum.

4

Our vet is called Mike Davis. He is small and dark-haired, with quick, sensitive hands. Wearing dark glasses, he drove into the yard in a brand-new Fiat. "And who would you be?" he asked David and Rachel, getting out of his car. Mum introduced them. Marli's leg had stopped bleeding and the sweat had dried on her, leaving white streaks.

"We don't know whether she's had her tet, and I don't suppose Maureen knows either," I told Mike. Mum fetched Angus a shirt, which he put on over his swimming trunks.

"We'd better give her a jab just in case," said Mike, feeling the wound. "It's not too bad. How did she do it?"

"She leaped a fence and hit the top rail. You could hear the impact half a mile away," Angus explained.

"She was all alone," I added.

"And came here in search of company," suggested Mike, filling a syringe.

"More or less."

I gave Marli a handful of oats while Mike slipped the needle into her chest, rubbing the place with cotton wool afterwards, muttering, "Whoa, take it easy. It's all right, pet."

"You'll send us the bill, won't you?" asked David Winter, leaning over the box door.

"Jean will give me your address. This horse needs to be turned out later. Standing still will only make her leg swell more. She should be all right in a couple of days," Mike told us, obviously assuming that Marli would stay with us. "She must come in every day until it's healed. I don't want her stamping," he continued. "Okay, Jean?"

I looked at David Winter. "Phantom will have to stay out then," I said.

"We'll keep her. Not to worry," said Angus, smiling at Rachel.

That is how we became friends, if you can call it friendship, with David Winter and his second wife, and Rachel Finbow.

We should have known better. We should have said, "No, we can't keep your mare. Send her to a posh stable where you will be charged sixty pounds a week. We haven't the room."

But Angus looked at Rachel and smiled – the die was cast.

Mike got into his car saying, "Call me if you need me," and glided away in the scorching heat, sweat glistening on his face.

"We can't keep her for ever," I said. "Sorry, but we haven't the room."

"We know that. You are a brick, Jean, the salt of the earth," David Winter said. "We won't forget it."

I believed him. But it was not as simple as that, nothing ever is. I wanted to keep Marli because I knew I would not sleep if she was in the railed paddock alone. Also, because we had let Rachel's mother buy the mare, I felt responsible for her safety. So I was caught in an impossible situation. Now it would be Phantom who had to stand alone under the oak-tree in the scorching heat.

Rachel and her stepfather returned to their car. "See you on Sunday. I look forward to meeting your husband," he told Mum, starting the engine. "And don't worry, Jean, you will be rewarded."

Rachel smiled at Angus and waved a small hand in my direction, while Phantom neighed despondently from the paddock.

"You must admit they are fascinating, Mum," Angus said. "Quite out of the ordinary. Nice too. Do you know what I had for lunch?"

"No," Mum replied, "and I don't want to. Your lunch here is wilting on the kitchen table. I don't know how we're going to cope with the mare. Jean has enough on her hands already."

Dad was not pleased to see Marli either. She was in the orchard by this time, her wound dusted with green antibiotic and fly-repellent powder.

"What is she doing here?" he asked.

I tried to explain. It sounded unlikely, as well as idiotic.

"You mean you helped them choose the mare for their daughter?" Dad asked.

I nodded miserably. There was a short silence before Dad said, "You're as idiotic as they are and, by the way, I would rather you didn't see too much of them."

"Why?" demanded Angus.

"Because they aren't our sort of people."

"Oh, I see. Their background is wrong, is it? Not Oxbridge I suppose," said Angus, in a cutting voice.

"Actually, he's Cambridge, and a scientist," replied Dad, taking us both by surprise. "She was married to a bomb disposal expert before he met an untimely death in the execution of his duty."

"I don't believe it. I don't believe a word you say, Dad," retorted Angus. "You don't like them because they are in business. You're inventing everything."

"You know he's not, but I don't think it matters," I said. "I don't like them either, but I'll have to look after Marli and teach Rachel to ride her, otherwise Marli will end up as dog's-meat."

"You could find her a better home," suggested Dad, walking into the cottage and slamming the door after him.

I do not like to recall the drinks party. Patio doors were opened on to the swimming-pool. We knew none of the other guests. David Winter introduced me as Rachel's friend. "A first-class rider and a real country girl," he added, patting me on the shoulder. There were eats scattered everywhere, drinks served from a bar by a man in a white coat. Halfway through,

David Winter led Dad away to look at the
equipment. A tall blonde lady asked me whether
I liked school, but after a few moments she lost
interest and turned away.

Rachel looked marvellous, and much older
than sixteen. Mum talked briefly about houses
and why she preferred the country to the town.
Angus followed Rachel from guest to guest as
though he were her private detective, while I sat
in a chair wondering why I was an outcast. The
air smelled of chlorine. I couldn't help wondering what the farmhouse made of it. Did it miss
the farmhands in their boots and Mrs Mooring
who had tended her cows in a long skirt and
overcoat? I wondered. But, of course, it was not
the same house now. The stone floors had been
removed or covered over; the fireplaces revealed
to be filled with flowers; the ancient kitchen
modernised; the old cooker gone; the pantry
now part of the kitchen; the scullery with its
old stone sink had become a utility room. There
was no hum of insects any more, just a contin-
ual murmur of equipment.

At last Dad returned, red faced, the sleeves of
his striped shirt rolled up. "Time to go home,"
he said. "Thanks for a wonderful party, David."

"It's a pleasure."

They saw us to our car. No one else was
leaving yet and I imagined them talking about
us afterwards and filling their glasses again.

What would they say? That Dad was intelligent, and the rest of us country bumpkins?

"What a party!" Angus said. "Well, did you like them, Dad?"

"Not particularly," replied Dad, sitting beside Mum who was driving.

"I feel drunk. I don't know what I drank. That man in white kept filling my glass," said Angus. "Wasn't the food terrific? You should be happy, Jean, with all the complimentary remarks you were paid on your riding."

"They were being kind. They had to think of some reason for my being there," I replied.

"I don't know why we had to leave so early. No one else was leaving," complained Angus, looking out of the back window. He was slurring his words.

I was disgusted.

Mum talked about the house. "They must have spent thousands on it. Do you remember how it was? You could have scraped the muck off the kitchen floor," she said.

Dad was preoccupied. The horses whinnied when they heard the car. Phantom was standing by the gate waiting to be brought in. Suddenly I felt like weeping.

"How much longer are you going to keep that mare?" demanded Dad angrily. "Can't you see she's eating all the grass? There won't be enough grass for our own animals soon."

Attempting to change the subject I asked, "What was the equipment like? Is it very up to date?"

"Too up to date," said Dad, stalking into the house.

Parties are supposed to be fun, I thought, tearing off my dress, which was blue and rather childish. What's wrong with us?

It was a cold lunch again, followed by coffee which Mum said we needed and, as we sat in the kitchen, I could feel the weather changing: a small wind made the checked curtains tremble, clouds fanned out across the sky. "We had better close the windows, it's going to rain," Mum said.

"What sort of equipment?" I asked again some time later.

"Computers, word processors, fax, that sort of thing, and things for tracking satellites," answered my brother promptly. "Rachel's shown it to me." Dad was in the garden. We could hear him attacking the weeds with a spade, using short, angry chops.

"I think I'll ride," I said.

"Me too," suggested Angus.

It seemed years since we had ridden together. By the time we were mounted it was spitting with rain. But when we returned everything was suddenly green again, the dusty flowers washed clean, the leaves on the trees sparkling. We were soaking wet, but there was a rainbow in the sky and I think we both felt better – Angus more sober, me more confident of my worth. We had talked only of Rachel and her parents, wondering what had brought them to Hill Farm House and how they had made so much money. We had discussed Rachel's character, Angus insisting that there was much good in it, I insisting otherwise.

"She says Dad's the handsomest man she's ever seen. She kept asking about him," said Angus.

"What did you say?" I asked, dismounting and running up my stirrups.

"I said that I couldn't really talk about his work, not that I know much about it anyway, and she understood immediately," related Angus happily.

"She is clever, you know. I know she looks dumb, but she isn't."

"I've never said she was stupid," I told him, letting Phantom go in the paddock. "All I've ever said was that she seems spoilt and that she's like a person wearing a disguise. She's selfish, too, because if she wasn't selfish, she would be here every day mucking out Marli, instead of treating me like a groom," I finished, suddenly unable to control a feeling of anger.

Two days later, Angus started work on Dominic's farm. Marli was now sound and Rachel appeared for her first riding lesson dressed in black denim jodhpurs and a black sweatshirt.

"I love black," she said, looking at me defensively. "And it doesn't show the dirt."

"But it does show white hairs if you ride a grey horse," I answered, laughing. "Angus, by the way, is working on the farm, so you won't see him."

"That's all right. I came to learn to ride, not to see Angus," she answered, offering Marli a sugar-lump.

Phantom was tied up in the yard. I had marked out a school in the paddock.

Rachel turned out to be better than I expected. She could rise at the trot and knew the basic aids. She could have managed a sensible middle-aged cob without any trouble, but was not up to a highly-strung Arab like Marli. I stood in the middle calling out orders: "Walk on. Trot on, square your shoulders. Hands still. Heels down. Don't lean forward. Tuck your bottom in. Prepare to halt." Gradually my teaching improved and soon I was enjoying myself. After half an hour I called a halt.

"I think that's enough for a first lesson, don't you?" I asked.

Rachel slid to the ground and started to pat Marli. "It was fantastic. The best lesson I've ever had. You're a born teacher, Jean," she said. "I mean it – a born teacher."

"You can do the same tomorrow if you like,

and the next day we might try a hack together," I suggested.

She gave me four pound coins. "I know it isn't nearly enough, but it's all I have just now," she said.

We turned Marli out so that she could roll, then went indoors for iced water and the flapjacks Mum was just removing from the oven. Then we sat in garden chairs on the small patio by the front door and Rachel said, "I envy you, Jean. I do really."

"Because I can ride?" I asked.

"No, because you have a brother and two parents, and because you've always lived in the same place."

"But no swimming-pool," I answered.

"But what is a swimming-pool? I would rather have your father than my stepfather any day."

"I'm sorry," I said.

"My real father was different. He was in the Army, quite high up actually. He should have sent someone else to defuse the bomb. He didn't have to do it himself." She was crying now, the tears smudging the mascara, her whole face suddenly crumpling, destroying the veneer which had been there before, so that now I could see the real face which was young and hurt and somehow, at that moment, defenceless. I did not know what to say.

"Did it happen a long time ago?" I asked.

"Three years ago," she replied, wiping her eyes on a handkerchief, "and Mother married David six months later, which made everyone talk. Of course, she knew him before. She had met him abroad when Father was posted to Belize. David wasn't so rich then, just a hanger-on really, the sort of person who does party rounds for the free food."

"I expect your mother needed someone," I suggested, feeling inadequate.

"You're all so honest, that's what I can't get over," Rachel continued. "Mother calls it being gullible. I mean, look at you looking after Marli for me. You don't have to, no one made you." She was standing up now. "Anyway, I must go. I have to man the telephone. I'm sorry about the outburst. Forget it, please. You won't tell Angus, will you? I haven't any other friends round here, only you and Angus."

"Okay. I won't. I promise," I said.

She visited Marli before calling, "See you tomorrow, then. Same time, same place, and thank you."

I kept my word and told Angus nothing of our conversation when he returned exhausted from the farm at half-past eight in the evening.

Rachel rode again the next day. I showed her various movements on Phantom first, like the turn on the forehand, the turn on the haunches and how to rein back. Then I cantered, asking her to call out which leg he was leading on. Then she rode Marli, sitting very still, having improved far beyond my expectations. Later, I lent her a pile of books to read and we sat discussing horses. She told me that her real father had learned to ride in the Army, and had planned to breed horses on his retirement.

"He would have liked you so much," she said.

Later still we cleaned the tack together and Mrs Parkin, whose day it was with us, said, "I'm so glad to see you two girls getting on together." There was a note of triumph in her voice because she felt responsible.

Later still, Rachel offered me a cigarette, which I refused.

"You're so sensible not to smoke. I know I shouldn't but it calms my nerves," she said.

She stayed to lunch that day, eating omelette and peas in the kitchen, followed by treacle tart.

"We have a conference, so I must go. I'm to serve the drinks," she said at three o'clock.

She had a bicycle now, a bright red one which clashed with the colour of her hair. She pushed four more coins into my hand. "See you tomorrow then," she called, pedalling away.

"You see, she's not so bad after all," Mum said, handing me a cup of tea. "Just lonely and mixed up, poor kid."

"But Marli will have to go back to Hill Farm House soon, because Dad's right – she's eating all the grass," I said.

"The Watsons need a home for their donkey. She could go up to Hill Farm House too, for the time being anyway, and keep Marli company. What do you think, Jean?" asked Mum.

"I think it's a brainwave! Well done, Mum," I cried. "I'll tell Rachel tomorrow."

We rode together the next day, letting our mounts walk through the valley on long, loose reins, stopping to wave to Angus and Dominic at work. It was cooler today with a wind blowing from the west.

Phantom and Marli were friends now; their strides matched perfectly, their manes rippled in the breeze, gold and chestnut.

"What would you do if Phantom suddenly died?" asked Rachel.

"Scream, yell, feel like killing myself. Honestly, it would take me months if not years to get over it," I said, leaning forward to pat Phantom. "But don't let's talk about such things."

"That's how I felt when my father died. Now I think I have a curse on me. I think people only have to know me to die," Rachel said. "Does that sound mad?"

"Yes, completely," I replied. I did not want

to listen but Rachel could not stop now. She had probably been bottling it up inside her for a long time.

"Uncle George died yesterday, he was my godfather, that's why I'm so upset. I liked him. He was a friend of Father's, not really my uncle. He had a heart attack. He went for a walk and died, just like that. One of my cats died the same way. My one and only cat actually. He went out and didn't come home. Now I fear Marli will die, or you," she almost shouted.

"Me? But my heart is all right. I'm young. I shan't die."

"Father was only forty."

"Well, I'm only fifteen," I snapped. "Let's trot. Use your legs, gently, hands still."

But as soon as we walked again, Rachel resumed her conversation. "Or your father could die. Then you would have a stepfather like me."

"Mum would never marry again," I said.

"Or Angus. He could get caught in a baler, it's always happening. Or you could all be wiped out in a car crash."

I put my hands over my ears and yelled, "Don't be so morbid. I'm not listening," and made a mad humming noise.

Then I looked at Rachel and saw that she was crying, the tears dribbling down her cheeks slowly, like eyedrops from a bottle.

"For goodness sake, we're having a lovely

ride. You're improving every moment. Whatever is the matter now?" I asked.

"I have a terrible sense of an approaching catastrophe. Don't come near me any more or you'll die. I know you will," she said.

I thought: She's mad. How awful. How terrifying. What can I do? The answer was nothing.

"You can have Marli back tomorrow. The Watsons want to put their old donkey in your paddock. She's called Maggie. Is that all right?" I asked, changing the subject.

"She will probably die, too."

"Stop being negative; be positive," I said, repeating something Dad is forever saying. "If Maggie dies it will only be from old age. She's reputed to be nearly forty."

"What a grand old age," replied Rachel, without feeling in her voice. "What's the time? We'd better move. I've got to man the telephone again."

"You seem to have a very important telephone," I said, pushing Phantom into a trot.

"It's business, and business reigns supreme in our house. Actually it's a call from the Middle East," said Rachel. "Most things come through on the fax, but this must be man to man for some reason, or man to poor little me. Maggie and Marli will go well together as names, won't they? Will you help me, Jean? Please? I do so love coming to your cottage and I don't want to give up my lessons."

"You needn't. We can still ride together and I'll help you."

"But it won't be the same, will it?" she asked.

"Nothing ever stays the same for ever," I answered, feeling overwhelmed and guilty at the same time for wanting a few days to myself to dream impossible dreams and to go down to the farm and see Dominic. "Of course we will see each other all the time. There's a marvellous horse show at the end of the month, with a class for Arabs that's just right for you. I'll help you practise for it, I promise. You don't have to cry," I said. "So do stop worrying. No one is going to die. We're all going to live to great old ages, even Marli and Phantom."

"How lovely to be so optimistic. I'm sorry to have been such a drip," said Rachel, dismounting in our yard and wiping her eyes. "I'm not usually like this. Please forget it, Jean."

But, of course, I could not forget it and dreamed that night that Dad was dying in a bomb attack on Sparrow Cottage. The whole house was in flames; no one could reach him. For a brief second we saw his face at a window, then he was gone, never to be seen again.

I wakened with tears streaming down my face to the sound of cocks crowing. Thank God it isn't true, I thought. But the dream stayed with me, the terror of it blocking out the dawn, continuing until Mum stood beside me fully clothed saying, "Wake up, Jean. It's nearly ten o'clock."

5

I dressed slowly, with Rachel's words echoing in my head: "I think people only have to know me to die." What did she mean? I wondered, pulling on my jeans. Surely she needed treatment. I hurried downstairs and stood in the kitchen saying, "I hope Angus is all right. Is he helping Dominic?"

"Yes, he went hours ago."

"And Dad?"

"You know he stayed the night in London. What's the matter, Jean?" asked Mum.

"Nothing. I just feel scared."

"But why, darling?"

"It's Rachel. I think she's mad," I said, before going outside to check on the horses. The nightmare was still in the back of my mind sending out tendrils of fear.

I stood patting Phantom while Mum called, "You can ride Marli over to Hill Farm House this morning. Mrs Watson is taking Maggie there about now."

"Okay," I shouted.

"What about breakfast?"

"I don't want any, thank you."

"You'll get anorexia nervosa, the slimmers' illness. You'll end up looking like a witch," said Mum, appearing with a bowl of cereal in her hand. "Now stop worrying about Rachel. She's a bit unbalanced, that's all. Take everything she says with a pinch of salt. I suspect she likes over-dramatising things and weaves fantasies. But that isn't insanity."

"Okay," I said, swallowing cereal. "I'll ignore half of what she says. I just hope it will be the right half." I could hear the combine in the valley. A few more days and the harvest would be in. It had been early this year and was breaking all records. Once it was in, Angus would be back at home and I reckoned I would feel safer with him around.

I gave Mum back the now-empty bowl. "You look pale, Jean. Are you sure you're all right?" she asked.

"I dreamed Dad was burned to death," I answered, fetching Marli's tack.

"You are in a mess, aren't you?" Mum told me. "Stop worrying."

"I'll try," I said, trying to smile. "I wish I could work on the farm. I need money."

"You can next year, when you're sixteen," Mum told me.

I led Marli out and, mounting her, waved goodbye. It was a muggy day without a breath of air anywhere, or so it seemed. The clouds were low overhead, the cow-parsley on the verges turning to seed. Suddenly summer seemed to be waning, the landscape wilting under the heat from the sun. "Be careful," I shouted to Mum. "Don't open the door to strange men. Drive carefully. Don't take risks."

"Oh, Jean, darling, I'm not an utter fool," she called after me. "Stop worrying, anyone would think I was a little girl. It's too stupid for words, you're not *my* mother, darling." She was still laughing as I pushed Marli into a trot.

I had caught Rachel's feeling of approaching catastrophe. What did she mean? I trotted on, not seeing the traffic, the road, not even Marli's pricked ears; riding automatically, my mind on Rachel. I wish I had never met her. I wish stupid Mrs Parkin had kept her mouth shut, I thought. What's wrong with me? Three weeks ago I was happy.

I could see the house now. Aerials, wires and masts, two satellite dishes, stark and alien in the Oxfordshire countryside. I thought of the room packed with equipment – the advanced computers, word processors, fax, all the latest gadgetry. I understood none of it, did not want to understand it, hated it.

I pulled Marli into a walk and could see Mrs

Watson in tweed skirt and pink jumper (in spite of the weather), holding a small grey donkey. The yard was crowded with cars. Music blared through open windows, drowning the country sounds and making a mockery of the birds' songs. I wish things never had to change, I thought. I wish Mrs Mooring was still here with her wild white hair, the yard full of squawking geese, cats everywhere and a smell of cow hanging over everything. Not forgetting the creepers covering the windows and the house looking so old with its crooked chimneys and sloping doors.

Rachel waved from the railed paddock and called a greeting.

I dismounted slowly. "You're still alive, then?" I asked. "Shall I let Marli go?"

She helped me take off Marli's tack, while

Mrs Watson stood admiring the house. "What a change. It doesn't seem possible, does it?" she said. I could see there was a new trough full of clean water in one corner of the field.

"Yes, it is changed," Rachel said. "The house is full of people, otherwise I would ask you in. Half of the visitors speak no English so I don't think you would like them much." She had dark shadows under her eyes and no make-up, looking physically and mentally exhausted. "I don't know how to thank you, Jean," she began.

"Don't then."

"Do you need a lift home?"

"I can walk."

I went home with Mrs Watson who talked all the way. "What a set up! They must be very clever people; like your father."

"Yes," I said. "They must be. But things around Rachel seem to die, so I expect Marli will die soon; she says there's a curse on her."

"Oh, for goodness sake, don't say such things," cried Mrs Watson. "Of course there isn't a curse. I've never heard anything so ridiculous in all my life. We're not living in the Middle Ages."

"Listen," I said. "Thunder. Do you think we'll be struck?"

"For goodness sake, Jean," exclaimed Mrs Watson, stopping at our gate. "What has come over you?"

I was like that all day. The storm came later, bringing Angus home on his battered old bike, soaked to the skin, calling, "We just cleared the eighty acres in time."

Dad was still in London. He was staying another day, and might have to fly straight to New York without returning home.

"Why? He's never at home now," I wailed, as thunder growled and lightning flashed in strange, jagged shapes.

"He's dealing with important government contracts," Mum said, but it meant nothing to me.

I thought of Marli standing in the railed paddock with Maggie, old and disreputable, beside her. They had nowhere to go, no shade, no shelter, no hedges, nothing. Donkeys are more delicate than horses, and Arabs are not like moorland ponies.

I stood at the sitting-room window biting my nails, watching the rain pouring down in torrents, bending what was left of the corn in the fields, whipping the petals off the flowers, flooding the gutters. It suited my mood, added to my feeling of impending doom.

But all things end. The sky lightened, the rain became a drizzle, the bent grass straightened and the puddles were suddenly lit by the sun. Mum opened the windows again while Angus wolfed enormous doorstep sandwiches.

       *   *   *

The next day I hacked with Rachel. She was riding well now and I had to admit that she was a quick learner.

"What a storm we had yesterday! One of our masts was struck by lightning. There was frightful bedlam."

"Have your guests gone?" I asked.

"Yes, all but two."

"Is Maggie all right?"

"Yes, fine."

We talked like that all during the ride, the conversation staying on everyday things: on school and approaching exams, on the village shop and Mrs Parkin. It was as though Rachel was making up for what went before, trying to tell me that she was really quite an ordinary person.

Angus was combining on the farm. Mum had gone to Reading. We put Marli in Killarney's box when we returned and drank mugs of coffee in the kitchen.

"I'm sorry I was so gloomy the other day. I miss my real father. You do understand, don't you?" she asked, taking her mug to the sink.

"Yes."

"I get depressed sometimes. But today was lovely. I really feel I'm progressing. Do I look better on Marli? Are my legs in the right place?" she asked.

"Yes. We must meet and practise for the show some time. I'll be your groom if you like; you know, go in when the saddles are off and flick a stable rubber round Marli. Mum usually does it for me, but somehow I don't think your mother will want to do it."

"Probably not. Thank you." We went back to the stable. I helped her tack up Marli. She was wearing no make-up, her hair was even tangled at the back, and her boots had mud on them. She looked normal and relaxed.

"I'm so glad we're friends," she said, mounting. "I must hurry because I'm supposed to be preparing lunch today."

Marli trotted away with an even stride, her head in the right place, her tail held at an angle befitting an Arab mare. I felt happiness come back, slowly, insidiously, until everything looked beautiful again. I'll tell David Winter to build a shelter for Marli and Maggie, to lay on a water supply. Then I won't need to worry until the winter, I decided.

Mum was back from Reading now, laden with shopping.

"All right?" she asked. "Better?" as though I had been ill.

"Yes, fine. I'm sorry I was such a fool. I don't know what got into me," I answered.

"I expect it was the thunder in the air. Can you carry the eggs, please?" asked Mum.

I took the egg boxes from the car while Mum said, "When are you seeing Rachel again?"

"I don't know. We haven't fixed anything up."

"You'll be able to help me then. I want to turn out some jumble for a sale in the village."

"But I was going to school Phantom, pull his mane and take his tack to bits, and whitewash the stables, tidy the muck heap and –" I cried.

"And, and, and," exclaimed Mum, laughing. "Come on, it's lunch-time and I've bought some ready-made lasagne."

Over lunch Mum said "You mustn't become like Rachel. Just remember you've had a secure and loving childhood, and your father is still with us."

"For the time being anyway. If he was killed, would you marry again?"

"I'm not discussing that. You are morbid. You grow more like Rachel every day. Help me find some jumble, then you can clean your tack and do what you want to do to the muck heap," said Mum, dishing out stewed apples.

It was a wonderful afternoon and a beautiful, peaceful evening; the last one we were to have for some time, but we did not know it then. Everything seemed drowsy that evening, slumbering, even the horses at peace grazing the dry summer grass.

I cleaned my tack in the kitchen, taking it to bits, cleaning inside the stud billets, noticing that my stirrups leather needed new stitching. Angus was too tired to do anything except idly turn the pages of a book. Mum made chutney. It was one of those evenings when life seems to last for ever, when change is unthinkable. Later the telephone rang. It was Dad saying he was being sent to New York. "It's only a flying visit," he said. He spoke to each of us in turn, which was unusual. "Don't go far, Jean," he told me. "Don't go alone."

"Why on earth not?" I shouted. "Can't I go out on Phantom?"

"Oh, you'll be all right on Phantom," he said. How wrong he was! Why did I fail to touch wood? But Sparrow Cottage has an aura of peace about it, feeling safe inside.

"By the way, the CID may call. They are still worried about the burglary," Dad told Mum.

Later we sat and talked, while darkness blotted out the orchard, the paddock and, last of all, the garden. A summer's darkness full of the sleepy voices of birds. Bats flew past the windows, an owl hooted. In the distance a cow was mooing.

"Why on earth the CID? We'd better tidy up," Mum said.

"Mrs Parkin is coming tomorrow. Have you forgotten?" asked Angus.

I opened my bedroom window when I went to bed and called out to Phantom and he answered, his neigh somehow muffled by the darkness. I could smell the roses still in bloom in the garden, and the sickly-sweet smell of honeysuckle.

In the morning there will be a mist, I thought. Cobwebs on the top of the hedge Dad has just clipped, the first dews of autumn.

Where was Dad now? I wondered next. Flying? Landing in New York? Already in conference?

I clambered into bed and sleep came quickly, a dreamless, carefree sleep. I did not know then that I would not sleep so well again for many a long night.

Next morning I rode again. Phantom was fresh, the morning mist soon cleared and the valley was suddenly empty without corn: a yellow wilderness which would soon become dark plough and then winter wheat. I galloped across the stubble and found Dominic and Angus tinkering with a vast machine.

"It's gone wrong again," said Angus, "and it's only a few weeks old."

"We ought to go back to horses," Dominic said.

I rode on and found Mrs Barnes was hanging out dusters in the yard by the farmhouse.

Mr Barnes was leaning over a door in the farmyard looking at a newly-born calf. Hens scratched near the house. A cock perched precariously on a gate and crowed. I galloped back across the stubble. The machine was working now, with Dominic perched inside wearing goggles, while Angus stood waving his arms in excitement. "Where's Rachel?" he asked me. "Don't you ride together any more?"

"I wanted to ride by myself, just for a change," I said, turning Phantom like a polo pony and galloping home. I hosed him down in the stable-yard and scraped the water off with a sweat scraper. I was so happy I could not help singing, but I can no longer remember what I sang.

Then Mum called, "Your father's just rung. He's in New York."

"Hooray," I shouted. "I think I'll ride Killarney after lunch. He hasn't been ridden for days."

We were halfway through lunch when there was a banging on the front door so loud that it sent tremors through the cottage. I rushed through the hall and shot back the bolts. Rachel was standing outside in riding-clothes, her face spattered with blood. For a moment I thought she was going to faint in my arms. Then she gasped, "Don't let them kill Marli." I helped her into the house and pushed her into a chair, while she said over and over again, "Where's Marli? Don't let them kill Marli."

"She's concussed," said Mum, rushing to the telephone. "Try to keep her quiet. Draw the curtains."

"But where's Marli?" I asked.

"It doesn't matter."

"It does."

Rachel refused to stay still. She was like someone demented, crying and screaming, "Don't let them kill Marli. Where's Marli, don't let them kill Marli . . ." In five minutes I wanted to scream too.

"Dr Cartwright says to take her straight to hospital," Mum said, looking for her car keys. "Shouldn't we ring her parents?"

"What's their number?"

"I don't know."

"Look in the book."

But their name was not in the telephone directory. Then we heard voices outside, and Angus calling, "We've got Marli. She's pouring with blood again. Where's Rachel?"

"Here. Concussed," I shouted. "Do you know her telephone number?"

Angus rattled off a number. Mum dialled it. There was no answer.

"We had better call Mike Davis again," said Angus, and I saw that Dominic was with him, in overalls and cap.

"She jumped off the track and got caught in the spike harrow. The harrow shouldn't have been there. It was my fault," he said.

Rachel looked at them, crying, "Don't let them kill Marli."

"She's outside. She's all right," I said, but it made no difference.

"You sit in the back with her," Mum told me. "I wish the doctor had called, she could do with a sedative."

We bundled Rachel into the car between us, while Angus shouted, "Shall I send for the vet, then?"

I shouted that old platitude, "Better safe than sorry."

Now Rachel changed her tune. "I want Marli," she said over and over again. Then, "Where is Marli?" as tears streamed down her face. "Where is Marli? I want Marli. Don't let them kill Marli . . ."

I put my hands over my ears.

There was blood on her hair, blood on her cheek, blood trickling down her black tee shirt. She must have hit the harrow, I thought, and then somehow found her way to us, more by instinct than anything else.

The hospital was crowded when we reached it. Nobody seemed perturbed by Rachel's repetitive cries. We were told to sit in a corridor and await our turn. Mum fetched us cups of tea, but we did not give Rachel any, afraid that she might need an anaesthetic. "She shouldn't have gone out alone," Mum said.

"Even if I was with her she might still have fallen off," I replied, trying to silence a feeling of guilt.

"Don't let her ride again on her own," said Mum, severely.

"She *is* sixteen," I replied. "She's not a little girl, she's older than I am."

Rachel was still talking like a tape in a continuous loop. A woman told us, "You shouldn't ride 'orses. They're nothing but trouble, start to finish, cluttering up the roads, eating good grass, spoiling the footpaths. Stick to your bike in future."

At last we were fetched by a bright young nurse and taken to a cubicle. I left Rachel there

with Mum in attendance. My head was aching and Rachel was still saying, "Don't let them kill Marli."

I sat on a bench with my head in my hands and I thought: It's all my fault. If I had ridden with her, if, if . . .

But when Mum reappeared a few minutes later she was smiling. "They're going to keep her in tonight, just to be on the safe side," she told me. "It's the best thing."

"So we can go home?"

"I don't see why not."

"Have you filled in all the forms?"

"I hope so. They will contact her parents," Mum said, running outside.

Mum was already in the car when David Winter stopped in front of me, his small eyes blazing, his huge eyebrows standing up like hackles. "Where's Rachel? What do you mean by bringing her here?" he stormed.

"She fell off Marli. She's concussed. We tried to get you on the phone."

He grabbed me by the arm. "And what has she said?" he demanded.

"Said? She keeps saying the same thing over and over; it's about Marli, nothing significant."

Mum was hooting the horn now.

A man in a scarlet shirt with bleached yellow hair and a chain round his neck asked, "Why don't you leave the kid alone?"

David Winter let go of my arm. "She'd better be all right," he said, swinging on his heels. I looked at my wrist: it was red where he had held it.

"What was that about?" asked Mum, leaning over to open the passenger door.

"Rachel. He's furious. Angus must have rung him. Mr Winter wanted to know what she said," I answered. "Look at my wrist. It's scarlet where he held it."

"I expect he was anxious. I would be if you went riding and didn't return. I'd be having kittens. And when men suffer they take out their frustrations on someone else," said Mum, starting the engine.

"I wish they had never bought Hill Farm House," I said next.

"They're renting it. It isn't theirs."

"But they've erected all those masts and things."

"I expect they're to impress customers. They're just glorified electricians and computer experts."

"But they're rich," I replied.

"Yes, they're clever businessmen, and not very honest either," Mum answered. "Anyway, they could be living on borrowed money, lots of people are."

When we reached Sparrow Cottage there were plainclothes policemen waiting for us.

"I hope it's all right. I let them in," Angus told us. "Marli's all right. It's just the old wound opened up again. Mike gave her a jab of penicillin. He says she'll be completely recovered in a day or two. How's Rachel?"

"Mad. Still shrieking. Did you ring her father?"

Angus nodded. "Her stepfather, you mean."

"He appeared at the hospital. He was in a terrible rage," I said.

We left Mum to deal with the plainclothes men and went outside. I fetched a body brush and started to groom Marli.

"David Winter slammed the receiver down on me," Angus said. "Do you think he beats Rachel? Batters her? You know, like you read in the papers?"

"Could be, and he's afraid she will tell someone at the hospital about it," I said. "That would explain his rage."

"And her fear, because it's obvious that somebody's been threatening to kill Marli, isn't it?"

I nodded and now I couldn't stop shivering.

6

The evening passed very quickly. I think we watched television. At nine o'clock Angus rang Hill Farm House, but there was no answer. At ten o'clock Dad called us.

"Is everything all right?" he asked, sounding anxious.

Mum told him about the plainclothes men. I told him about Rachel. Angus merely called, "Give him my best wishes," in a silly voice.

Another night came upon us, with more terrible dreams, followed by a wet morning.

"I think we should go to Hill Farm House. Will you ride over on Phantom?" Angus asked, standing by my bed fully dressed.

"And take Marli with you," called Mum from the passage. "We don't want to be accused of stealing her."

So later we tacked up our horses. The rain had stopped. Angus had dusted Marli's leg with the green powder which was antibiotic and fly-repellent.

"Hurry up. I'm working after lunch," he said.

Killarney was full of bucks and shied at every heap of earth and dustbins. I led Marli on the outside of Phantom. We had put on her tack, but her new saddle was scratched and her reins broken at the end.

"Rachel wasn't wearing a hat. You know that, don't you?" asked Angus. "We looked for it and Dominic promised to bring it over if he found it."

"That explains the state of her head," I said.

"It does, doesn't it," said Angus, nervously adjusting the chinstrap on his own cap.

We trotted up the hill, Marli and Phantom going beautifully together, their strides matching, Killarney cantering sideways.

Maggie hee-hawed from the railed paddock. She looked old and anxious, the house looked deserted.

"Where's Rachel?" asked Angus, with anguish in his voice.

"Still in hospital," I answered, to soothe him.

"One day they'll batter her to death. She'll be found at the roadside and there will be a full-size murder hunt," he said, gloomily surveying the house.

"Why will they kill her?" I asked.

"I don't know. I wish I did," replied Angus, dismounting.

We let Marli go. She would not leave us, neighing piteously as we put the tack in the porch by the back door. The house was locked up, even the swimming-pool was deserted. I know because I held the horses while Angus searched the premises for some sign of life, returning to say, "We had better ring the hospital."

"But we're not relations," I said.

"I don't care. I shall ring anyway." There were tears in his eyes, which he pushed further in with his fists, like a small child does. "Stop staring," he shouted. "What's there to stare at?"

"Nothing," I answered, leading the way down the drive.

"I have sixty pounds now. I was going to ask her out, take her somewhere smart. I was thinking of asking you too, and Dominic . . ."

"How kind."

"Anyway, there's a good film on tonight at the Odeon in Reading. Dominic wants me to go with him, will you join us too? It might cheer you up. There's a horse in it . . ." Angus said.

"Thank you," I said. "Of course I will. It's years since we've been to the cinema, and it might cure the nightmares I'm having every night."

"Dominic will pick us up at seven-thirty then," Angus said. "Then we can see the whole programme – okay?"

"Perfect."

"If Rachel is back I'll invite her," said Angus, ever hopeful.

"If Rachel is back she will be keeping quiet for two days at least," I answered. "She won't be watching anything much. She was very badly concussed. Much worse than you've ever been."

I read a book after lunch but, although it was a murder story and exciting, the words failed to penetrate, so that five minutes later I could not remember what I had read.

Phantom kept neighing for Marli and I wondered whether the flies had found their way to her wound yet.

Mum rang the hospital for Angus, who stood over her biting his nails. "She's still there, she's comfortable," said Mum, replacing the receiver.

"What does that mean?" demanded Angus.

"Nothing, but obviously she isn't dying," Mum said.

At six o'clock Angus returned from the farm and stood in the hall calling, "Any news?"

"No, nothing."

I had turned Killarney and Phantom out into the paddock and changed into a denim skirt and cotton shirt. I had cleaned my shoes and was suddenly glad that I was not competing with Rachel, who I imagined appearing decorated with an array of jewels, her nails gleaming, her tawny hair gleaming, eye-shadow round her extraordinary eyes.

At seven-thirty Dominic drew up outside our gate in the Land Rover. "Hop in," he said, holding the door open. He had slicked down his hair and was wearing a suit and a tie with horses on it. He looked as though he was pretending to be someone else. Angus was wearing jeans, cracked brown shoes and a thin polo-necked jumper.

"Any news of Rachel?" asked Dominic.

"None at all, not a word," replied Angus.

"What about the mare?"

"She's back with the Watsons' donkey," said Angus.

"It was a lucky escape. She could have broken her leg in the harrow. I'm still kicking myself," Dominic said, driving on to the main road.

The film was about the Cavaliers and Round-heads. Both sides rode so atrociously that they set my teeth on edge. We had popcorn and Cokes and ice creams during the interval.

Dominic refused to let me pay for anything. "This is my treat. It's not often we go out together, Jean," he told me firmly.

When we came out of the cinema, Angus said, "We can't go home yet. It's only ten o'clock. Let's have something to eat."

"What about Mum all alone in the cottage?" I asked. "Anything might happen."

"You're becoming like an old woman," retorted Angus, angrily. "All you ever do is worry."

"Jean can telephone, there's a telephone in the Indian restaurant. Let's go there," suggested Dominic. "Here, Jean, I have some change. I know how you feel. My mother will be worrying too."

The meal was a long time arriving on our table. I nearly fell asleep waiting and forgot to telephone. The boys talked about Rachel, then about the farm and about the new machine.

We arrived home in the dark. One of the horses neighed. "We ought to check them," I muttered, still half asleep.

"They're all right," replied Dominic, turning off the engine.

"It's misplaced maternal instinct. Jean's turning Phantom into her baby boy," said Angus, laughing. Since working together, Dominic and Angus had become firm friends; they had jokes I did not understand, knew people I have never met. Now they sat in the kitchen drinking coffee until two in the morning. I sat with them, not wishing to be left out.

Mum appeared in her dressing-gown, asking whether we had had a good time.

When Dominic left, the first sign of a summer dawn was spreading across the sky. Killarney neighed. "They're missing Marli," said

Angus, yawning. "They'll get over it."

How was I to know then what was to follow? That every misdemeanour has its price? I fell into bed and my eyes closed instantly. I have no recollection of any moment between sleep and Mum rapping on my door calling, "Phantom's gone. He's not there. There's only Killarney."

I fell out of bed and pulled on clothes, shouting, "Where? How? It can't be true." Daylight flooded the room. "They were neighing. We should have looked."

"You mean Killarney was neighing," replied Mum.

"We should have looked. I knew we should have looked," I yelled in anguish.

Then Angus appeared, looking dishevelled and still in his pyjamas, saying, "Calm down. He's probably gone to see Marli."

"Along the main road," I shrieked, thundering down the cottage stairs. The kitchen clock told me it was ten o'clock. Panic rose in my throat. Why did I oversleep? I thought. But I knew the answer already. We had stayed out late, had not checked the horses, been selfish, hopeless . . . Killarney stood by the gate, neighing frantically when he saw me, imagining that I could wave a wand and Phantom would return. Or did the sight of me merely bring hope?

Angus stood beside me now. "You look down the road, while I ring up the abattoirs," he said.

"The abattoirs?" I screamed.

"Yes, he may have been stolen," he said, with awful calm.

I ran down the lane and called to old Mrs Cannaway in her flower-bedecked garden, which is so wonderful that she opens it every July in aid of the Red Cross.

"Have you seen Phantom?" I shouted. She put down her secateurs.

"Phantom, dear?" she asked.

I saw that she did not belong to my world,

for her world was governed by begonias and
bulbs, by crocuses and snowdrops.

"Yes, my horse."

"No, dear."

I was already running on. The main road was
full of traffic – thundering lorries, salesmen driving too fast, women on their way to shop.
There was no sign of Phantom, and if he had
been there, it would have been as minced meat
on the tarmac . . .

I returned home. Angus was talking to Dominic on the telephone. "He's coming over
immediately in the Land Rover. We're going to
do a clean sweep. Have you got a headcollar
and oats?" he called.

Mum was ringing up the police station as we
fled the cottage.

"What about the abattoirs?" I asked.

"I rang three. I warned them not to destroy
him. One manager said there's a sale on Saturday we ought to attend," replied Angus.

"Saturday?" I yelled. "But he must be back
by then."

"We'll go to Hill Farm House first," Angus
told Dominic through the Land Rover window
when he arrived in overalls, still bleary-eyed
from the night before. "Phantom may have gone
to see Marli."

"Surely the Winters would have telephoned?"
suggested Dominic.

"They're hardly ever there," Angus said.

"Don't worry, Jean. He'll turn up; he's probably having a rare old feed of grass somewhere at this very moment. How did he get out?" Dominic asked, starting the engine as Angus slammed the passenger door.

"We didn't look."

"You should have done. You don't want Killarney out too," Dominic said a minute later, driving full speed along the lane.

"No, we don't. But he could have been stolen, couldn't he?" I asked.

"Didn't you hear anything? What about your mother?"

"She was watching television, and our walls are thick," I said. "And you know we were out till nearly midnight."

Dominic hooted at a lorry which had stopped on the hill.

"We were amusing ourselves while he was being stolen. It's awful, isn't it?" I said.

"He may not have been stolen. We have no proof," replied Angus.

"Let out, then?"

"Or escaped."

Mr Winter was in the drive at Hill Farm House. Marli was grazing beside Maggie, there was no sign of Phantom.

"I'm not speaking to him, not after how he treated me," I said.

"We must ask after Rachel," replied Angus, getting out and then standing in the sunlight smiling. Meanwhile, my heart grew heavier with each passing moment.

"How is your daughter, sir?" asked Angus.

David Winter was quite civil. "She's gone to London with her mother," he said, smiling.

"She's better then?" asked Angus.

"Yes, much better."

"Have you seen Phantom? He appears to be lost," asked Angus next.

"No. I am sorry though. As you can see, all is quiet here. Perhaps he will return at feed-time. Horses are creatures of habit, you know. They like routine. Alter a horse's routine and he's bewildered," said David Winter, smoothing his hair with plump fingers.

"He's setting up as an expert on horses now," I told Dominic. "I wish Angus would hurry. Time is running out. I feel every passing minute is one lost, and every hour will be like a defeat."

"Oh, Jean, don't carry on so; he's only a horse after all," replied Dominic, patting my knee. He sounded like his mother, tiny old-fashioned Mrs Barnes, who is always pickling, or jam making.

I wanted to cry, but couldn't because some things are too bad even for tears, and losing Phantom was one of them. As Dominic started the engine I could see, with terrible clarity, my life without Phantom – his empty box, his un-used tack, the cavaletti decaying, the dressage signs disintegrating, because if Phantom was lost for ever I would not ride again. I vowed it now sitting between the boys on that hot August morning gritting my teeth.

"What next?" asked Dominic.

"A wider sweep," said Angus.

We must have covered miles. We stopped at farms, at riding schools, at every place where we could see horses. We asked a crowd of ram-blers, a milkman, a woman pushing a pram. "Have you seen a loose horse by any chance?" The reply was always the same. Not once did anyone offer us a single grain of hope.

"He seems to have disappeared from the face of the earth," announced Angus at eleven-thirty.

"If he escaped at eight o'clock last night, he could be miles away by now," said Dominic.

"If he was stolen, he could be in Scotland, or dead by now," I said, swallowing tears.

"Let's go home," said Angus.

Mum was manning the telephone. "Any news?" I shouted, rushing into the hall.

Shaking her head she said, "Not a sign, Jean." Dominic looked in. Mrs Parkin was shaking mats.

"I must go. I have ten acres of corn still to be cut," he said.

"We can't thank you enough," said Mum.

"He'll turn up. I know he will," Dominic said, without much conviction in his voice. "Not to worry, Jean."

We watched him go in silence. Then Mum put the kettle on.

I sat down in the familiar kitchen and I wondered what Rachel was doing in London; what she would say when she heard about Phantom. I wished Dad had returned. I wished I had never been to the cinema.

"Here, drink this, you look terrible," said Mum, handing me a mug of tea. "He'll turn up, darling, don't worry. It's early days yet."

"We'd better search the woods. Angus, can I borrow Killarney?" I asked.

"Help yourself," he told me. " I'm going to phone the auctioneers about the sale on Saturday. It's mainly carriages, that sort of thing, but there are some horses."

"But driving horses?" I asked.

"Yes, mostly, but it's worth trying."

He looked tired, too. On edge. Was he blaming himself? I wondered.

Returning to the kitchen a few minutes later, he said, "They have a late entry; it's entered as a cream gelding of fourteen-two, so it could be Phantom."

"When was it entered?" asked Mum.

"This morning. But no address was given. It

was a call from a call-box apparently, and the caller ran out of money."

"What about age?" I asked, my heart pounding in my chest.

"Eight years, and some people call palomino cream," replied Angus, staring out of the kitchen window as though all the secrets of the world lay outside on the flagstones. "I know, it's all my fault. I shouldn't have stopped you looking at the horses last night," he added disconsolately.

"It wouldn't have made much difference. He would have been gone by then. I heard a lorry in the lane around ten o'clock. I remember now," Mum told us. "I thought it must be going to the farm, and Killarney neighed soon after and, like you, I thought he was neighing for Marli, so I was a fool, too." I saw Mum was crying, the tears washing away the make-up on her face.

"The interesting thing is that the cream horse was entered late as one of a pair," Angus continued. "That explains several things."

"Such as?" I asked.

"Why Killarney was left behind."

"You mean someone wanted a match for their cream or palomino?" I asked.

"Yes, there doesn't seem to be any other explanation, does there?" said Angus. "If Mum heard a lorry, he must have been stolen. Also, if he was going for meat, why not take Killarney who is much easier to load, much heavier and so worth more."

"I'm not giving up the search. I am still going out on Killarney," I answered.

"Pairs of palominos are rare," said Angus, thinking out loud. "They must be, mustn't they?"

Although I knew it was not true, I had not the heart to contradict him; besides it was a crumb of hope, and I needed hope. I imagined the sale. I imagined Phantom standing tied in the long shed. In my mind I heard him whinny. It was something to help me through another day, a sort of crutch to lean on and, though he had never been in harness, it might still be possible.

7

In the woods in the autumn the fallen leaves crackle under a horse's hoofs. Today Killarney's hoofs made no sound on the damp earth. I leaned down searching for other hoofprints: smaller, neater ones. There were none. I stopped at every fence to search for golden hairs, asked Killarney for his opinion and let the reins fall on his grey neck saying, "Take me to Phantom." But after a moment he simply turned for home. I reached Maureen's stables and found her grooming a bay hunter.

"Any luck?" she called.

I shook my head. "Don't give up hope. He'll turn up. I'll keep an ear open. I'll ask around."

But I knew that minutes later she would have forgotten.

"How is Marli?" she asked next.

"Still alive."

I did not want to talk about Marli. There was only one thing I wanted and that was news of Phantom.

"Have you rung the police?"

"Of course, and all the abattoirs as well," I answered, turning Killarney round.

"I'm sorry," she said again. "But if you don't find him, I promise I'll find you something else."

"I don't want something else, I want Phantom," I shouted, riding on to the road. "There'll never be another Phantom."

Killarney is the kindest horse I know. Phantom shows off, moves with a flourish, bounces underneath you, sometimes his hoofs hardly seem to touch the ground. Killarney has a marvellous long, even stride. His head is steady, his ears a long way off. He is a large high-powered station-wagon, while Phantom is a sports car, zippy, quick to accelerate, easy to turn.

It was dusk when I returned home. I did not even ask for news as I dismounted in the yard, for I knew there was none by the silence which lay over everything like a reproach. Killarney was missing Phantom, too. He looked across the paddock, ears pricked, then sighed and looked mournful.

I turned him out and he whinnied, then walked up and down alongside the fence, then whinnied again. If Phantom does not return, it will be the end of an era, I thought, trudging indoors where Mum looked at me and, saying nothing, held out a mug of tea. What was there to say? Absolutely nothing. In my mind, I was beginning to accept that I might never see Phantom again. The sale was our last hope, and what a hope! I thought before asking, "When does Dad return?"

"Sunday, probably on the afternoon plane."

"To Heathrow?"

She nodded.

"Is that definite?" I asked.

"As definite as anything ever is," said Mum.

I cleaned Killarney's tack, playing my cassettes full blast to drown my feelings. Angus was oiling his bicycle again.

"Tomorrow we go to the sale," he shouted, and then, "I think somebody is tapping our telephone. Did you know?"

I switched off my cassette player and stared in disbelief. "Are you sure? But why on earth?" I asked.

"That's the million-dollar question."

"Have you told Mum?"

"Not yet. I don't want to upset her. It's probably MI5. Dad's been doing some pretty secret work lately," replied Angus.

"Personally, I wish he owned a shop; then we could earn money helping and he would be here all the time," I said.

"What sort of shop?" asked Angus, laughing. He lifted his eyes heavenwards as though calling upon God to witness my stupidity.

"A tack shop, of course, which he could take to shows," I shouted, elaborating. "In a horse box which we could use as well. We could also buy all our clothes cheap, then I would be even smarter than Rachel Finbow."

"You couldn't. Whatever you put on you'd never look like Rachel," said Angus, seriously. "You'll always look like a country girl and, if you had tea at the Ritz, oats would fall out of your pocket when you took out a hankie to blow your nose. Your shoes would leave Oxfordshire mud on the exquisite carpet and . . ."

"I don't want to go to the Ritz, and I don't want to look like Rachel," I interrupted, angrily. "I'm happy as I am, and I'm going to build a better world for horses, and that's far more important than how you look," I finished.

"Listen! Telephone!" shouted Angus.

I rushed indoors and, snatching up the receiver, covered it with a thin layer of saddle soap. But it was only Dominic asking, "Any news?"

I couldn't keep the disappointment out of my voice as I answered, "None, absolutely none."

"Angus says he may be at the sale tomorrow in the market. I can't go but, if he does, I'll fetch him back in the trailer. You know that, don't you?" Dominic asked.

"If he goes. Thank you, thank you very much." I put the receiver down slowly and, as I did so, there was a strange click. Now, as tears gushed down my cheeks, I knew I didn't want to think about Phantom any more.

I slept badly with muddled dreams where Phantom and Dad were both on an express train hurtling towards a precipice, and I could do nothing but watch. I got out of bed and saw the dawn break. Killarney was lying down by the gate of the paddock; there were rabbits everywhere and a hedgehog walking across the paving stones below the window, and the honeysuckle clinging to the wall smelled like sweetened incense. At ten to seven I took Mum and Angus cups of tea in bed.

Mum was sitting up reading a detective novel. "Oh darling, how lovely," she cried. "I couldn't sleep. Could you?"

I shook my head. "Today is our last chance. If we don't find him today, I don't believe we ever will," I said.

"You mustn't give up," Mum told me. I saw that her hair was going grey on top, where once it had been a glowing brown. "We'll find him even if it takes months."

"I don't see how," I said, shutting the door after me.

"Why so early? The sale doesn't begin till ten. Are you insane or something? The palominos will be sold last, because they're late entries," Angus said, taking his mug of tea.

"I don't care. I want to be there when they arrive," I answered. "They may be sold privately, you know, on the side. Phantom could be whisked off to Scotland, to Poland; people visit sales from all over the world."

"They would never get Phantom on to the plane. God knows how they got him into the horse box in the first place," Angus replied.

"I think the police should be helping us more," I said. "They're not doing a thing."

"They're keeping an open mind. Go out please, I want to dress," said Angus, throwing back his bedclothes.

Mum drove to the horse sale. I was wearing my dark glasses again, and it seemed years since we had been there with Rachel. We were far too early, but horses and vehicles were already arriving and there were driving enthusiasts everywhere, many with foreign accents.

I hurried from horse to horse with Angus in tow complaining that I was making an exhibition of myself, that I was making people stare and that there was no point in hurrying anyway. Mum stood talking to complete strangers about Phantom. Soon I was feeling sick with apprehension, knowing that if Phantom did not show up, I would lose all hope of ever seeing him again.

We watched each horse box and trailer arrive and each one unloaded. At times the suspense was unbearable. Some of the horse boxes carried driving vehicles inside and others Shetland ponies. But there was no palomino or cream horses to be seen. Nothing but blacks and bays and a dashing pair of greys.

Then, at twelve o'clock when the sale was half over, a cattle truck roared into the market and stopped so quickly that we could hear the horses falling about inside.

"This is it!" I exclaimed. "It must be."

I felt sick. I clambered on to the wings and looked inside, but all I could see were two heads raised in fear. Men pulled down the ramp. The horses wore headcollar-ropes and were ungroomed; they could have been stolen. The way they had arrived seemed to confirm this, but they were cream and not palomino, and neither of them was Phantom.

"We may as well go home," I said, feeling faint with disappointment, everything seeming far away and then coming closer until I wanted to scream because the whole air was suddenly suffocating. Mum took my arm to stop me from falling. Angus ran ahead to open the car door.

"All this for nothing. The whole morning wasted when we could have been looking, telephoning people. Why did we bother?" I asked, sitting in the back of the car.

"Because we hoped he would be here," Angus replied.

Mum turned the car slowly, her hands white-knuckled on the steering wheel. "We'll find him in the end," she said without much conviction. "Don't give up hope, Jean."

We found Rachel waiting for us at home,

sitting in one of the garden chairs swinging her elegant legs.

"They've found Phantom," she told us. "The police rang. I had no idea he was lost."

"Where?" I shrieked. "Where is he?"

"Near High Wycombe. Get a map," she said, smiling at Angus. "I hope you didn't mind me answering the phone," she added. It was only later that I was to wonder how she had entered the cottage which we had locked so carefully on leaving.

"We'd better phone Dominic. It's too far to ride Phantom. Are the police quite certain it is Phantom?" asked Angus.

"Yes, but you can check. It's the local police station."

I ran to the stable for a headcollar and oats while Angus rang the police. "It sounds right," he said, on my return. "He's palomino and he was grazing on Southend common. No one seems to want him."

"Where is he now?" I asked, my hands shaking.

"Shut in someone's farmyard."

Ten minutes later, Dominic appeared with the trailer hitched on to his Land Rover crying, "Oh, Jean, I'm so glad. Hop in."

"I told the police we would be there in forty minutes," Angus said.

Rachel squeezed in between us. There was no

room for Mum now in the front of the Land
Rover, but she said, "Not to worry, I've got
plenty to do at home."

It was now past lunch-time and none of us
had had any lunch.

"Well done the police," exclaimed Dominic.

"Are you better, Rachel? When did you return home?" Angus asked.

"Ages ago. I've been in London since then,
I've bought a present for you," she said, handing him a pair of gold cuff links in an ornate
little cardboard box. "I am getting you something, too, Jean, and you, Dominic," she said.

"How is Marli?" I asked, changing the subject as I did not want a present from someone I
did not like much at the moment.

"All right. I called to see when we could ride
together."

High Wycombe was full of traffic and all the
lights were at red. I started to bite my nails,
while Angus and Rachel talked about London, a
place Angus hardly knows but which he talked
about as though he lived there. Dominic turned
to smile at me and his smile seemed to say,
"Are you happy now?"

So I said, "Yes, thank you."

Then we were in the suburbs, and soon driving along a country road with grass verges and
straggly hedges. My heart was thumping against
my sides like a sledge-hammer.

"Third time lucky," Angus exclaimed.

"Is it the third time? Touch wood anyway," I answered, touching my head. I could hardly bear to look now.

Dominic knew the farm. "I once fetched two pigs from here," he explained, stopping outside a pair of iron gates tied together with binder twine. A police car was parked at the roadside.

"That was quick," said a policeman, with a small moustache. Then, "Follow me."

I do not know how to describe the next few moments. The yard was empty concrete, no Phantom; but beyond lay a smaller enclosure which had probably once been a straw yard full of calves. But now the animals were kept in larger, newer buildings, in what are called "units", where they can be under strict control and fed hormones, steroids and tranquillisers, or so Angus says, and in this smaller yard was a palomino, which turned its head and whinnied at me, its eyes flooding with hope, its ears pricked. But though it looked so like Phantom and welcomed me, it was not Phantom.

This time I did not feel like fainting. I simply felt numb all over, as I stood there saying nothing, while everyone seemed to be staring at me with hope in their eyes, the policeman even taking my headcollar from me and advancing on the horse.

I found my voice at last and said, "Sorry, it's

another mistake. I'm sorry we brought you all this way, Dominic. It isn't my horse," and my voice did not sound like me.

"Are you sure? It looks like Phantom," Rachel replied. "It must be him. Look again, Jean."

"She's right," Angus replied. "It's Phantom's twin, but it isn't Phantom."

We thanked the police and returned to the Land Rover.

"We'll pay for your petrol, and what about your time?" Angus asked Dominic.

"Forget it," Dominic replied, looking at me.

"Next time we'll check it out better," Angus told him.

"There won't be a next time, and it's no good pretending there will be," I answered. "Forget telling me not to give up hope, and don't say, 'Where there's life, there's hope.'"

"Don't say anything, in fact," suggested Rachel, to which I made no answer.

As we travelled home, it seemed to me that all my troubles had been brought about by Rachel's arrival. Until then I had been happy, my future mapped out, no shadow of fear on the horizon. Now, as I looked at her rather thin face and at her eyes, where there seemed to lurk a glimmer of madness, I hated her. But I said nothing and probably appeared to be sunk in abject despair whereas I was now overcome by an intense dislike and an unexpected overriding anger, so that I turned to Rachel, unable to contain myself a moment longer, and demanded, "What made you decide to live in Oxfordshire? Why didn't you stay in London?" Angus put up a hand as though to shield her from the venom in my voice.

"I don't understand, Jean," Rachel replied,

unperturbed. "What is it you are trying to say?"

"Nothing. She doesn't know what she's saying," interrupted Angus. "Ignore her."

High Wycombe was still full of traffic and it was now unbearably hot in the Land Rover. Rachel asked for a cigarette. Angus gave her one, which surprised me because Angus does not smoke.

We could now see the hills of home, and Dominic, patting my knee, said, "If you never find Phantom, we'll find you a wonderful new horse instead, an Anglo-Arab as fast as the wind, Jean."

"Thank you," I replied stiffly, because I was holding back my tears. "Phantom is as fast as the wind. If I never find him I shall give up riding."

"You see how mad she is," commented Angus. "She's totally unreasonable. He's only a horse after all, but because he's vanished, we must live in eternal mourning."

"That's not fair, Angus, and you know it isn't," replied Dominic in a level voice. "Jean loved that horse, didn't you, Jean? I know what it's like to lose an animal you love. My first dog died when I was eleven years old and I shall never forget it."

"Well, Phantom wasn't a dog, was he?" said Angus.

They're talking about Phantom as though he's

dead, I thought, as we drove towards Sparrow Cottage. They are making him into history. Soon they'll be saying, "Do you remember when Jean had that horse called Phantom?" But we don't know whether he's dead yet. We may never know. He could be anywhere by now. He could be being whipped, or ridden to death; or be travelling towards some distant foreign abattoir or sold as a riding horse but travelling in the hold of a ship, starving, thirsty, rocked from side to side by rough seas. Oh God, let him be dead rather than that.

Mum ran out to greet us. "How is he? Is he hurt?" she asked, surveying our blank faces with concern.

"It wasn't him, and it never will be him," I answered, pushing past her and running up the familiar stairs to my room, slamming the door and locking it before falling on to my bed to give way to a flood of unstoppable tears.

8

Some nights seem endless, while others disappear in dreamless sleep. I refused supper. I refused a hot malt drink. I refused a glass of milk and sandwiches, ice cream, trifle, even apples. You may think I was exaggerating my grief, but it was not like that. The thought of food made me feel sick and for an hour or two I did not even wish to go on living. In vain Mum tapped upon my locked door saying, "Jean darling, there's no point in locking yourself in. It won't bring Phantom back."

I knew it was true, but could not help myself. I think I wanted to hurt someone because I felt hurt myself and the nearest person was Mum. She lost patience with me in the end, saying, "Don't eat anything then," and went downstairs where I could hear her talking to Angus and Rachel in the kitchen; not the actual words, more the hum of voices. I hated myself for being so unpleasant.

As I have already said, sleep did not come

easily that night. I heard Killarney whinnying for a lost Phantom. I heard the mournful hooting of a solitary owl. I heard Mum locking up, calling goodnight to Angus, then adding, "Don't worry, darling, Jean will feel better in the morning."

I heard a car going down the lane, voices, silence, the bark of a distant dog. Through the darkness I could just make out the shape of trees. I thought dawn would never come. I slept fitfully. The night was of the endless variety, dawn a long time coming and with it unwanted sleep, and that the next thing I knew was Mum knocking on the door saying, "We've got to go to the airport soon. Are you coming?"

I sat up and called, "No, thank you."

"It would do you good."

"No thank you."

"We're fetching Dad. He's coming into Heathrow," Mum said.

"Good for you. I hate Heathrow."

Then Angus stood outside the door saying, "Must you be so horrid? I'm going with Mum. Don't you want to meet Dad?"

"No, and there's no point in my getting up either," I answered.

I looked at my clock. It was eleven o'clock. Normally, at that time, I would have leaped from bed and, pulling on clothes, rushed outside to see Phantom, but there was no Phantom, only Killarney – and he belonged to Angus.

Mum returned once more to my door to ask, "Did you give Rachel a key to the back door, Jean?"

"No."

"How did she get one then?"

"I have no idea."

"You won't be coming with us then?"

"For the last time, no."

"Do be careful then. Don't do anything silly," she told me. "And keep away from strange men."

"For goodness sake, I'm not six years old," I said.

I heard the car start up, the crunch of tyres on gravel. I got out of bed and drew back my curtains. The day was sunlit, the grass dry, with only the buzzing of insects to break the silence.

How *did* Rachel get a key? I wondered. How did she answer the telephone when we had locked up on leaving? I ate bread and cheese and drank a mug of tea. I found the emptiness of the cottage soothing. I'm not going to give up, not yet anyway, I thought. I imagined Phantom returning, his box ready for him, Killarney neighing. If only it could happen.

I walked through the village and kneeled in the small grey church which I had entered only once before and asked God to give me back Phantom. It was very quiet in the church. No one answered, but no one laughed either. There were cobwebs in a corner and one of the stained glass windows was cracked. When I reached the cottage again it was half-past twelve and the telephone was ringing. For a moment I was afraid to pick it up, then I put out a hand and, holding the receiver to my ear, said, "Hello?"

The call was from a call-box and, while whoever it was pushed coins into the coin box, I imagined Mum and Angus broken down on the motorway or Dad standing at one of the telephones at Heathrow saying, "I've arrived."

But in the end it was a strange male voice which asked, "Have you lost a horse?"

Suddenly my voice seemed to have gone and I could only whisper, "Yes."

"He's up on Hell's Hill above the Devil's Churchyard," the voice told me. "He's been there several days by the look of it."

"What does he look like?" I asked.

"The same as the one I've seen you riding."

"I don't know who you are," I said.

"It doesn't matter. Can you get there? Have you got any transport?"

"No, but I can use my bike. I'll be there in twenty minutes," I shouted. "Will you wait?"

"Will do," the voice answered.

The back tyre on my bike needed pumping up.

I found the map and saw that the Devil's Churchyard was nearly five miles away.

I almost rang up Dominic for help but decided that we had bothered him enough already, and now I was glad I had not gone to Heathrow. I thought that God had answered my prayer as I fetched Phantom's bridle, and, mounting my bike, I thanked him silently in my thoughts.

The lane was hot and dusty, the main road hotter still. I rode fast, pedalling like a maniac. I'll phone home, I thought, when I've got him. There's sure to be a call-box and won't Angus and Mum be surprised! I started to sing. Lorries hooted at me and a man opened a truck window to call, "Do you want a lift? Hang on the back." I shook my head for I had no intention of speaking to strange men.

There was a long, steep hill with woods in the distance, yellow and emerald. My legs ached, my head pounded. I stood on my pedals. I'll leave my bike when I get to the Devil's Churchyard, I thought. We can pick it up later in the car. I'll ride Phantom home bareback. I hope he's all right. Cars passed me, throwing dust into my eyes, and at times the sun was blinding. But the woods beckoned me on, though for ages they seemed to grow no nearer.

The Devil's Churchyard is a gloomy place. There are no graves, but maybe the dark yews

which grow there gave the place its name. Or maybe there was a macabre story connected with it.

I threw my bike down, hung Phantom's bridle round my neck. A bird wheeled in the sky. Sheep grazed, penned in by old-fashioned hurdles. There was a smell of thyme. I felt the place had not changed in a thousand years.

As I climbed the hill I could see the distant Thames dotted with boats, and a railway line with a long train winding along it like a snake; and from distant chimneys there was smoke in the sky hovering as though undecided which way to go. Insects were everywhere, bumble-bees and ants, wild bees and butterflies all leading their own intricate lives. The ground was dry, the sparse grass wiry.

I was wearing jeans and my favourite checked shirt. Sweat ran off my face and my legs ached. But soon I could see a cluster of buildings, then a horse, unmistakably Phantom, tied to a fence. I then began to run, stumbling over ant-hills, my heart pounding louder than ever, and now I was seeing my triumphant return home – Killarney neighing, Mum, Dad and Angus, perhaps even Rachel, laughing with joy.

Phantom's bit banged against my chest as I ran. Wild flowers twisted themselves round my jodhpur boots and I kept saying, "Thank you God, thank you." Then, having no breath left, I slowed to a walk and the hum of insects was suddenly deafening in the silence. I could see the buildings properly now; an old, disused yard with nettles growing where once animals had stood, a cottage with smashed windows, red bricked, unused, unwanted, like a disreputable vagrant, no electricity wires, the remains of a rougher time . . .

I stopped to call to Phantom, then, as he raised his head and whinnied, I could see that his sides were run up and that his mane was tangled with parts of it missing. There were weals on his quarters which could only have been caused by whips, and his dear face was black with flies and his quarters had hollows in them which had not been there before. But at least he was alive!

But he knew me. Life came into his eyes; he pawed the earth and waited whinnying, his eyes pleading for help, while mine were suddenly full of tears, half joy, half pity.

I shouted again, "Phantom, just a minute. I'm nearly with you, wait for me, Phantom," and I hardly knew what I was saying, so intense was my feeling of joy.

I fetched oats from my pockets, held out my hand, saw a horse box parked in the yard, saw men emerging from the buildings, not one but three. My spine started to tingle and my whole body to shake for they were all strangers with stocking masks on their faces, and one of them carried a gun . . . They fanned out around me as though I was their quarry while I shouted, "I've only come for Phantom. Leave me alone, please leave me alone."

Although I could not see their faces, the way they moved was enough to tell me that they were enemies; no doubt the strange men I had been warned against time and time again. Quickly I looked round for help, but only the insects were there and Phantom, and now the men were closing in while I ran straight to Phantom yelling, "Help me, Phantom, help me."

He was tied by a strong rope hooked over a post. I lifted it and sprang forward. A few years back I had been considered for the Prince Philip Team and a girl called Alison had taught me to vault on to my pony Mermaid at full gallop. Now Phantom was galloping and I shouted, "Wait for me, Phantom," and then with one terrific leap I was on his back, urging him on. I was clinging to his mane, my knees tight against his sweaty sides.

A motor-bike started up behind me, and below me lay the road winding into the distance. We leaped an ant-hill, then swerved to avoid a rabbit-hole. Phantom was out of control. He was fleeing and I was fleeing with him. I don't think either of us knew where we were going.

Now the motor-bike was roaring behind us, trying to cut us off from the open gateway below. We were going faster than I've ever ridden before, with fear giving strength to Phantom, whose hoofs hardly seemed to touch the ground, while his tangled mane lay damp against his neck and his neat ears were flat against his head.

I thought that when we reached the gate I would be safe. I thought that the long straight road below would welcome us, that there we would find cars and people who would save us. But, as we drew near, I saw a Mercedes draw up across the entrance, and it rang a bell in my mind which went on ringing; then a man stepped out and put binoculars to his eyes, while I screamed, "Help! Please help." As I drew near, I made out the figure of Mr Winter and I started to wave and shriek, "Help me, Mr Winter, I'm being pursued. Please help."

He stood in the field and said, "Oh, it's Jean, is it? Just jump off and I'll take care of you, dear." He smiled, a smile which stayed on his lips and never reached his eyes.

"I'm not leaving Phantom," I answered, while the man on the motor-bike drew alongside, sweat running down his neck from beneath his mask. He nodded at Mr Winter, and then words came back to me, things Rachel had said and which I had not believed at the time, but which were now bits of a puzzle that slotted into place.

The man on the motor-bike dismounted and took off his helmet. He was quite young and his hair was dark and curly, while his hands were large and red – butcher's hands, I thought.

"Did you hear what I said, Jean? Get off. Phantom can find his own way home," shouted Mr Winter in a voice which was used to being obeyed. He was no longer smiling, rather his eyes seemed to have grown smaller, his beard larger, his accent more foreign.

Meanwhile, poor Phantom stood with his head hanging low and his sides going in and out like bellows.

"Stop pussyfooting. Pull her off, Sid," David Winter said. "Go on, put the bike down."

I turned Phantom round then and, leaning

forward to grab the top of the headcollar, I
pounded him with my legs while I heard David
Winter shout, "And shoot the damned horse if
necessary. I don't want her to get away . . . Do
you hear, Sid? She's not to get away. Kill the
horse if you like, but get the girl . . ."

I knew the other men were waiting for me by
the old buildings and I knew that one of them
had a gun. The motor-bike was revving up now,
leaping into action, hurtling over the rough
ground, gaining on us. I knew that it would not
tire like Phantom, that it could go for hours
without a break. There's no hope now, I
thought. I wondered why I had not left a note,
just the words: *I'm going to the Devil's Churchyard to fetch Phantom. Jean.* Just that might
have saved me. But I had left nothing, not the
smallest hint of where I was going. It is on such
small things life depends! Not mine alone, but
Phantom's, too.

A man by the building raised his gun and
fired, which made Phantom flee faster, while I
lay low on his neck saying all the prayers I
knew, which are few, but in a way they were
answered, for now I realised that the wood was
our only salvation. I turned Phantom with difficulty and at the same time heard the motor-bike
revving up and someone yelling, "She's making
for the woods. Cut her off, Sid."

Then we were racing neck and neck straight

for the dark woods, for the trees which had stood there for hundreds of years and for whatever lay beyond. The motor-bike leaped over the ant-hills which were everywhere, its exhaust filling the air with fumes, its roaring engine drowning all other sound, even Phantom's breathing which was growing laboured while, panic stricken, I could feel the pounding of his heart.

Once the motor-bike swerved in front of us but Phantom swerved faster, then we were in the woods. Branches tore at my shirt and pulled my hat from my head, twigs stung my eyes, and we could still hear the motor-bike engine close behind, while the sky was blue above us still. I knew that the wood did not last for ever, that soon we must reach the other side and maybe a fence against which we could be cornered like rabbits, taken prisoner for what purpose I had no idea and did not have time to contemplate, for now all my thoughts and strength were needed to stay on Phantom; to save myself from being swept off him by branches and to save my knees from being smashed by tree-trunks, to save us both somehow.

We came to a wire fence and beyond were fields sloping gently to the river, but there was no way round the fence, no open gate, no wide, inviting track. I let Phantom walk along it, my heart hammering, my eyes seeking a way through and, all the time, the sound of the motor-bike was growing nearer, its fumes overpowering the smell of trees and earth. Now sweat ran down my face in a torrent, while my legs felt limp, and my eyes were full of bits of tree, and my hands scratched and bleeding.

My parents would be home by now, they had to be, I decided. They would be out looking for me, standing in the road most likely. Wondering. Ringing Dominic. No one would know where I had gone. I had been told a thousand times never to go out alone without leaving a message to say where I had gone. I could not forgive myself for forgetting.

There was the sound of voices which meant that the other men were catching up with the motorcyclist. Another minute and they could be firing at Phantom, aiming for his legs, even aiming to kill. I pushed Phantom on with my legs. Ahead of me I could see nothing but conifers, thick, dark green and almost impenetrable. Behind me were the men on foot and the motorcyclist. Their voices sounded cheerful now, while my heart was sinking. I was filled with an appalling feeling of helplessness. Then I saw the stile. It was narrow with two steps and made of roughly hewn wood, and I turned Phantom towards it, trying to collect him between my legs, crying, "It's our last hope Phantom. You must jump it. If you don't, we're finished . . ."

133

Then I was riding him forward, holding his mane in my hands, and he almost stopped. Then we were over and galloping on. Now fields lay below us to the river, and just before the river was a house and a yard, the sort of yard you dream about, with loose boxes in a rectangle, with grass in the middle and five-barred gates leading off into railed paddocks. There were people like tiny dots down by the river. I recognised the yard, but between us there lay a cross-country course with a variety of fences I had never jumped before. All the gates were padlocked. I knew the yard was my last hope, for now I could hear the voices coming out of the wood. The sun had moved so that it shone straight into our eyes. There were sheep in the first field, which scattered at our approach. Sheared, tidy sheep without lambs. Tall trees along the banks of the river cast shadows on the water.

I galloped on, listening for the roar of the motor-bike behind, recalling the Carruthers family who owned the yard ahead of me. They were ardent pony clubbers, every Pony Club cup had one of their names on it. They were rich, too, and I was about to jump their cross country course. There was a shout and I looked back and saw that the men were heaving the motor-bike over the stile and that one of them still had a gun.

Suddenly my legs were turning to jelly and I was riding as I had never ridden before, down the hill towards a brush fence as high as Phantom's ears . . . I tried to collect him, but he was too much on his forehand and he was very tired. I had never known him so tired before. Without impulsion or much spirit, he was no longer the fiery Phantom whom I loved. I seemed to be holding him together with my legs and my hands on the headcollar-rope, and I had the feeling that if I let go he would simply fall apart.

There were three fields to cross before I
reached the safety of the yard so I was praying
again as we approached the brush fence which
looked so neat and civilised. I was praying that
Phantom could jump it and carry me on down
to the safety of the yard. I could hear the mo-
torbike starting up, and the sound sent a cold
feeling of fear down my spine. I held on to
Phantom's mane and drove my knees into his
sides. Then we were over and galloping on, and
by now the people on the river were no longer
dots in the distance but real men, women and
children. I knew that the motor-bike could not
jump the brush fence and that the gates were
padlocked. Leaning down, I patted Phantom
saying, "We're almost safe, Phantom, just carry
me a little further."

Then I could hear the voices on the river, and
saw a figure sitting on a stool fishing. Then we
had reached the next fence which was high and
wide and complicated. I did not know how to
take it, whether it was one or two fences, and
my head was pounding again and my heart
racing. Now I could not stop Phantom. He was
in control, galloping full speed, his weight far
forward, his breath coming in gasps, and all
my strength seemed to have gone. I grabbed the
top of the headcollar and shouted, "Whoa,
Phantom, steady . . . Whoa," but all to no
avail. Suddenly I knew with awful certainty that

we could not clear the fence. I tried to turn him sideways. I pulled so far that the headcollar went over his eye so that he could not see on that side, and then the headcollar came off altogether. Now there was nothing I could do but hold on to his mane and pray. Then I saw that it was two fences and I shut my eyes and prayed. Some moments are long in one's memory, some short. This one cannot have been more than a few seconds, but it seemed to last for ever . . . A dozen images flashed across my mind – the men scooping me up while Phantom lay with his neck broken; my parents searching for me; Angus exclaiming, "Why didn't she leave a message? Is she mad?" The men in masks carrying me to a car, the smell of the chloroform. Sparrow Cottage without me or Phantom, my empty bedroom.

Then we hit the fence, stars flashed and wood splintered before my eyes; voices shouted in the distance. I felt Phantom keeling over, and threw myself sideways before I hit the earth with a terrific thud, which seemed to reverberate through my entire body; then I was crying, "My back! Oh, my back!" trying to move and feeling sick. Phantom was struggling to his feet and the voices were coming nearer. I did not know whether they were friend or foe . . .

9

I stood up slowly, the landscape spinning before my eyes. The house below lay slumbering in the sun. The voices belonged to the people on the river. The men in masks had gone. "Are you all right, love?" asked a man who put his arm round me to help me up. He was strong and middle-aged and wore a yachting cap.

"Yes, it's just my back."

"Do you want an ambulance?"

I shook my head saying "I've got to get my horse."

Someone said, "She's a game one!" and someone else, "She needs a doctor."

My back was still hurting and through the pain I said, "I have to go to the house down below. I know the people there. I must send for the police."

"Someone's doing that just now. We saw them chasing you. Don't you worry, love. Why don't you rest?"

But I could not rest, not with Phantom gone,

and all that had happened. At this moment I was certain I had to go on to the end.

"I'm going down the hill to the house." My legs moved and every step hurt less. The middle-aged man came with me while the others went back to the river. I could not see Phantom any more.

"Why were they after you?"

"I don't know. One of them was supposed to be a friend."

"Some friend. Where are your parents?"

"On their way back from Heathrow."

"You'll have to have an X-ray. I'm not sure you should be walking at all," said the man.

"It's hurting less and I don't feel sick any more." The man took a gate off its hinges to save me from climbing it.

Now I could see the yard dotted with people, and Phantom. I wished I could run. Then people started coming up the hill towards us calling, "Jean, are you all right? What happened?" I wished I could run to meet them.

The man called, "She's hurt. It's her back. She shouldn't be on her feet."

Mr Carruthers, who is tall and lean, called, "Shall we bring a hurdle, Jean?"

I called back, "No, thanks. How's Phantom?"

"Bloody but unbowed."

"Bloody?" I yelled.

"Yes. Jonathan is ringing the vet now. I

presume Phantom's had his tet . . ."

"Yes." It hurt to talk. Sometimes it hurt to breathe. But every step was one step nearer to safety.

I looked back and my enemies had gone, and all the landscape was quiet and calm. Even the birds were quiet, while down below the posh yard was swept clean, the centre grassed over and bright with flowers, the house newly painted, an elegant car parked by the front door.

I could see Mrs Carruthers waving, coming up the hill towards me, then Mr Carruthers was with us, saying, "Shall I carry you, Jean? You can't weigh anything."

I said, "No, thank you. I don't want to be bent," and both the men laughed.

"She was being pursued, we've sent for the police," said the man in the yachting cap. "They were firing at her. I've never seen anything like it in my life."

"They wanted to kidnap me. I don't know why. We have nasty neighbours you see, and Dad's work is hush-hush," I said.

"Are you sure you're not concussed," asked Mr Carruthers, smiling gently at me.

"Absolutely certain."

"Well, you do seem to be talking absolute rubbish."

"I saw her being chased with my own eyes,"

said the man from the river. "I couldn't believe it at first. The men were wearing masks. It was like something on telly."

"You'll be a witness, won't you?" I asked. "Because I'm going to need witnesses."

"Of course I will, love."

"There's the vet," said Mr Carruthers. "You can't grumble about that for speed, can you?"

Mrs Carruthers brought a chair out and I sat in the yard while the vet examined Phantom, who seemed to have blood mixed with sweat all down his legs. Now I felt very cold.

Alison Carruthers, who's seventeen and a top rider, fetched me a mug of tea with sugar in it. Mrs Carruthers wrapped me in a rug, while Mr Carruthers rang up home and the man from the river stood watching, not sure whether to go or stay.

Then the vet, who was about forty with brown eyes, looked at me saying, "He's in a terrible condition, Jean. What have you been doing to him?" I tried to explain but none of it seemed to make sense, except that the man from the river, who turned out to be called Alan, kept confirming it. When I had finished the vet said, "I think you should send for the police."

"That's been done," said Alan. "As soon as we saw what was going on my wife took the bike and went to the nearest kiosk."

"Has he had his tet?"

I smiled at the vet and said, "Yes, he's up to date." Marli's had her tet too and so have I, I thought, so we are all in the clear.

"Okay. He'd better stop in tonight. Have you a box?" asked the vet.

"No trouble," said Alison. "I'll just get some straw."

"I'll give him a vitamin injection, and some penicillin just in case. He doesn't need stitching," continued the vet.

Jonathan, who had been holding Phantom all this time, exclaimed, "Thank God for that."

I could not look at Phantom because every time I did I wanted to cry. He looked so forlorn, so broken down, as though I had been riding him to death for weeks instead of for minutes.

"Okay, Jean, we'll see to Phantom," Jonathan said. "You go in and rest. You look as though you need it."

"I'm sorry," I replied. "I didn't mean it to happen like this."

"Of course you didn't, darling," said Mrs Carruthers. "We're only too happy to help you."

"The vet will send the bill to us, won't he?" I asked.

"Yes, of course."

The house smelled of furniture polish and flowers. In the hall Alan said, "Well, goodbye, all the best, Jean. I can see a police car down by the river so I'll scoot," and held out his hand.

I said, "I don't know how to thank you. I think you saved my life. I expect we'll meet in court." His hand felt hard and warm.

"All in a day's work, Jean," he answered, and was gone, running towards the river, silent in his trainers.

"I hate not being able to help. I would like

to look after Phantom," I told Mrs Carruthers, who had followed me inside.

"Don't be ridiculous. This will stop you shivering, Jean. What on earth were you doing riding hatless and with nothing but a headcollar?" she asked, handing me a drink.

I said, "It's a long story. Can it keep?"

"Yes, of course, darling. Your parents will be here soon."

"They were at home then?"

"Yes, just arrived."

I imagined them arriving, the telephone ringing, Dad suffering from jet-lag, Mum exhausted by the traffic around London.

"What a homecoming. Were they cross?" I asked.

"Of course not."

"Phantom won't eat. I'm giving him a mash. Is there anything he particularly likes?" asked Alison, standing before me in jeans and a green shirt.

"Grated apple."

"Okay, I'll do my best."

There was the sound of tyres on the gravel outside. Then Dad, Mum and Angus came rushing into the house like a whirlwind, and I said, "I'm sorry I've been such a nuisance, but Mr Winter and his friends wanted to kidnap me."

Dad said, "Yes, I know. The police have most of them in custody."

"And Rachel?" I asked through chattering teeth.

"She's at our house."

"How did you know?"

"Rachel told us. We kept ringing to see if you were all right, and you weren't there. You see, Dad's plane was delayed," explained Mum. "We were torn apart. I was so afraid something had happened to you, and yet we had to meet the plane."

"I'm sorry," I said again.

"You should have left a note," said Angus.

"Then we found Rachel waiting for us, shaking like a leaf. She threw the door open and screamed, 'They've got Jean and Phantom. She's gone to the Devil's Churchyard,'" Mum continued her explanation.

"She was a heroine," said Angus. "I know you never liked her, but you were wrong, Jean."

"I like her in bits," I said.

"David Winter was using her as a pawn," said Dad.

"I always knew there was something wrong," I told him, while Mr and Mrs Carruthers brought us soft drinks. Then Alison reappeared to say, "It's all right Jean, Phantom's eating."

"What about the police?" I asked.

"I saw them on the way. They were by the river," Dad said, sipping apple juice. "They're calling in the experts – the Special Branch."

I lay back in a chair while the adults talked; then Dad said, "Come on, we must get back. We've left Rachel."

Then I cried, "Where's Rachel? Why is she in our house?"

"It's a long story. We'll tell you in the car," Dad said.

"Her own house is full of police," Angus told me. "She has nowhere to go."

"What about Phantom?"

"We'll look after him, Jean," said Mr Carruthers, his arm round my shoulders. "Not to worry, Alison has just got her H certificate and Jonathan is training to be a vet. When he's better we will box him over to you."

"Yes, home will be the best place for him," agreed Jonathan, who was tall like his father, with a long, straight nose and greyish-blue eyes and dark hair – a real Celt, Mum said later.

"But he won't box."

"Then I'll lead him over off one of my horses, no problem," replied Alison quickly, smiling at me. "They need all the exercise they can get."

"I don't know what to say."

"Don't say anything then."

Angus was talking to Alison now, asking about the approaching long-distance ride; and the sun had dipped below the river and nearly all the boats had gone. I stopped to speak to

Phantom. He was standing at the back of an enormous box, resting a leg, wearing a posh checked rug.

"Don't worry, Jean. We will look after him and send him home to you good as new," Jonathan said.

"They kept him in that ruined yard above the old churchyard with nothing to eat for days and not much to drink either," I told him.

"Yes, our vet said he was dehydrated, but he'll get over it. He's a wonderful little horse. When we saw you coming down here, we couldn't believe it – bareback, without even a headcollar; it was unbelievable. At first we thought it was a stranger. Then we saw it was you, riding straight at the fence and we just held our breath and prayed."

"So you saw me approaching?" I asked.

"Just the last bit. Then Alan rushed up from the river panting like mad and Phantom came into the yard half dead, steam rising off him in clouds, his sides going in and out like bellows. We thought he was going to drop dead in the yard. We all started screaming at each other like lunatics – ring the vet, ring the doctor, help Jean, see to Phantom . . . What an evening!"

"Thank you anyway," I said.

Dad was hooting now. I climbed into the car slowly, and waved and waved.

"You like him, don't you?" asked Angus.

"Who?"

"Jonathan."

"Who wouldn't?"

"He's a real sweetie, a real Celt," Mum said. "A lovely family altogether."

"We used to think they were stuck up," I remembered. "But what about Rachel? Why is she in the cottage? You haven't explained anything properly."

"It's a long, long story," Dad replied.

"I think she's having a nervous breakdown, actually," said Angus.

"Is she alone?"

"No, Mrs Parkin is with her."

"Mrs Parkin?" I shrieked so loudly that it hurt my back. "Why Mrs Parkin?"

"Because there was no one else and we couldn't leave her on her own," said Mum wearily.

"Why didn't you leave Angus?"

"I thought you might need me," Angus replied. "I thought I might have to bring Phantom home."

"We've all got a lot of talking to do. Leave me at the top of the lane and take Jean to the surgery," Dad told Mum. "Angus can come with me and get dinner, and don't argue."

"There are chops in the fridge, ice cream and lots of fresh veg in the larder, and soup in a tin," Mum told him, changing seats with Dad.

"Do I really have to see the doctor?" I said.

"Yes, just to be on the safe side," replied Dad, climbing out of the car and taking his case with him, looking incredibly tired, so tired that for a moment he swayed on his feet . . .

"My hat is in the woods," I said, as Mum turned the car. "I'm sorry to be such a nuisance. Is Rachel really ill?"

"I don't know. She was screaming and incoherent. She answered when we rang – but we were ringing for nearly two hours before anyone answered. What a terrible day it's been!"

"What did she say when she answered?" I asked, leaning over from the back seat.

"She said that you had been kidnapped and that we must hurry. We didn't know whether to believe her or not. It was terrifying. Your father drove like a madman; don't ever let me hear you say he doesn't love you again, because it simply isn't true. Of course there were roadworks on the M4, so we drove through Slough, and then back on to the M4 near Maidenhead. Dad was hooting at everyone and Angus was screaming in the back. If only you had come with us."

"Then Phantom could have been dead," I said slowly. "But I still don't understand why I was kidnapped."

"All will be revealed tonight," said Mum, parking the car.

149

Dr Richardson was in his house when we knocked. He appeared and unlocked the surgery saying, "Not another riding accident?" before telling me to bend over a chair, then feeling my back until I screamed.

"Okay," he said at last. "You can stand up again. I'm absolutely sure you have cracked a vertebra and there's nothing we can do about it; just try to walk straight, don't stoop, and I'll give you some pain-killers."

"How long will the pain last?" I asked.

"About six weeks."

"And she's not to ride?" asked Mum.

"Better not," he said, handing me a bottle. "Take two, four times a day."

"Is that all then?" I asked.

"Yes, unless it gets worse. Then come back and we'll have you X-rayed. But I thought you were a good rider, Jean?"

"It's a long story," I said.

"She's lost her hat too, she might have been killed," Mum told him. "Thank you for seeing us.

"Come on – home. What a day it's been," exclaimed Mum as we got into the car.

I thought of Phantom standing in his enormous box, looking forlorn, lost and thin, oh, so thin. I won't be able to ride him for months, so we'll be invalids together, I thought as we reached the lane, which seemed to me then the most beautiful lane on earth, and Sparrow Cottage dreaming in the dusk looked like paradise.

10

Mrs Parkin was sitting in the kitchen, and stood up as we entered. Dad was on the telephone. Angus was washing lettuce at the sink.

"How is Rachel?" Mum asked, shutting the back door after us.

"Asleep, poor kid, worn out. Whatever will become of her?" asked Mrs Parkin, looking for the mackintosh she always wears outside, winter and summer, wet or fine.

"How much do we owe you?" Mum asked.

"Nothing, absolutely nothing. She says her horse is dead. She says Mr Winter shot 'er. She 'eard the shot. What a terrible business."

"What, Marli?" I cried.

"The one you found 'er."

"Angus, do you hear? Marli's dead!" I shrieked.

"There's no need to shout. If she's dead, she's dead. It's a quick way to go, one shot straight through the brain. Better than the abattoir, she won't have known a thing," he said, shaking lettuce in a tea-towel while I sat in a chair and started to cry.

"I've made a salad to go with the chops. They're in the oven and I've done some potatoes," he told Mum. "Anything else you want?"

Mum laid the table while I stayed in the chair, feeling too weak to do anything. I seemed to have lost all sense of time. I saw that the clock said eight-thirty now, but eight-thirty what? Was it Saturday or Sunday?

Dad was letting plainclothes policemen through the front door. Then he opened the kitchen door to call, "Sandwiches and coffee, please," as though we ran a restaurant.

Mum fetched a sliced loaf from the bread-bin and asked Angus for some lettuce leaves while I repeated, "Marli dead? I don't believe it. I simply don't believe it."

"David Winter was a spy, you realise that. He was trying to sell secrets. Trade secrets, defence secrets. Whole systems. Communications too, secret ones. He was a traitor. He wanted Dad's secrets. He was using Rachel. He was the burglar, or his accomplices were," Angus told me, dishing up chops.

"How do you know?" I asked.

"Rachel told me before you came back. When she had told me she went to bed. She said she couldn't sleep until she had told someone. He had to get one more plan, and then he

153

had the whole damned system, and Dad had the plan. You were to be ransomed for it; that's why he kidnapped Phantom."

"It could be fantasy," said Mum calmly. "Sit down and eat."

"Why didn't she tell us before?"

"She was too scared. Marli's life was at stake, even her mother's. Her father had tapped our phone, that's how he knew when we went to the airport. He was getting desperate . . ." continued Angus.

"They kept Phantom a long time," I said.

"Rachel didn't know they had him, not at first; then she overheard something and as far as she was concerned from then on it was you and Phantom, or Marli and possibly her mother, and she chose you . . ."

"I saw David Winter and I thought he was a friend. I rode right up to him and he called me 'dear'," I remembered, shivering again.

"Dad says you won't be needed as a witness, because they've got enough evidence. He wants to keep you out of it, but I think you'll be needed for an attempted kidnapping charge," said Angus, happily.

"Have the police got both the Winters, then?" I asked.

"Yes, both of them."

"Who will look after Rachel?"

"Her granny. She's got a granny," Mum told

me. "The mother of her real father. She lives in Hampshire. She's arriving here in the morning."

"Does Rachel know?"

"Yes, we fixed it before we fetched you, because the Carruthers, bless them, said that you and Phantom were okay, so we thought we had better deal with Rachel first. Her granny sounds a real honey," Mum told us.

Suddenly I could not eat any more. I was now unexpectedly and overwhelmingly sorry for Rachel. "It's all such a mess," I said wearily. "There's Rachel having a nervous breakdown, Phantom ill, me with a cracked back and Marli dead. And all for what?"

"It was all for money. The Winters had bought tickets to go abroad somewhere," Angus said.

"Was Rachel going, too?"

"Yes. She didn't have a choice."

"But surely they could have been extradited, couldn't they?" I asked uncertainly.

"I don't know, it depends where they were planning to go," Mum said.

Angus was stacking the plates now. He seemed to have grown older and more sensible.

"Dad's going to be hours with the Special Branch. Do you think we could go and look at Marli, because if she's dead we must get the horse slaughterers," he said.

"Yes, and poor Maggie must be so upset," I agreed. "We must go."

"You can stay here if you like," Angus said.

"I want to go. My back is hardly hurting. I'll just swallow a couple of pain-killers," I told him, standing up, finding my legs were wobbly, opening the tablet bottle, taking out two tablets and swallowing them with water.

"Supposing Rachel wakes up?" I asked.

"She won't; she's dead to the world," said Angus.

"I'll just look and make sure," I said, creeping upstairs and looking into our tiny spare bedroom where Rachel lay sucking her thumb like a small child. I went downstairs again and out into the garden.

"Rachel's all right," I said, getting into the car with difficulty. "She looks years younger, quite different actually."

"Like she was once," Mum said, starting the engine.

It was almost dark, but the lights were on in Hill Farm House and there were police cars parked in the drive.

Angus had brought a torch.

"We mustn't be long," Mum said.

"Why don't you stay in the car, Jean?" suggested Angus. "You know you'll only cry."

"I'm all right," I replied obstinately, trying to ignore my aching back.

Then I started to call, "Marli, Marli, where are you?"

Angus said, "You're crazy. She's dead. We are looking for a corpse."

I said, "Do you think Maggie is dead, too?"

"Don't make such a noise. We don't want the police out here," Mum told us.

Then I heard a movement in the grass and I

thought: It's Maggie! but then I saw neat chestnut ears and a large eye and I said, "She's not dead after all."

I held out my hand with a piece of bread in it and Marli took it.

"Thank heavens for that!" exclaimed Mum.

I held my breath while Marli took another piece of bread and Angus shone the torch on her and we saw that she was quite unblemished, while Maggie stood behind her like a humble servant.

"He must have done it to frighten Rachel. To make her turn back," said Angus, who is not short of imagination. "What a wretch!"

We went back to the car. I was crying again, half joy, half exhaustion.

"We'll have to wake up Rachel and tell her," Angus said.

"Not tonight. I can't stand any more tears. I'm totally exhausted," insisted Mum, turning the car. "Tell her in the morning."

"Not if she's awake," said Angus.

"Please God she isn't," replied Mum.

The Special Branch men were leaving as we arrived home. Killarney whinnied to us from the paddock.

"Well, what happened?" Mum asked Dad.

"It's all right. We're in the clear."

"Will they go to court?" asked Angus.

"Yes, of course, but thank God we got them

in time. Thank God you didn't let them catch you, Jean. I don't know what I would have done if they had. I really don't," cried Dad.

"Gone to the police, of course," said Angus.

"I don't know. I suppose so. But it wouldn't have been easy," Dad said suddenly, bending forward to kiss me. "My God, it wouldn't have been easy. But Jean was too smart for them, weren't you, Jean?"

"No, it wasn't like that. It was Phantom who saved me. He was fantastic. But then he *is* fantastic, whatever you say. A horse in a million."

"Let's go to bed. I'm drooping," suggested Mum. "We can sort everything out in the morning. What's that man doing at the gate?"

"He's guarding us, just in case," Dad said.

I do not know how long I slept. I woke to the sound of Angus singing tunelessly below my window. The sun was shining outside and I opened my window to call, "Why didn't you wake me? How is Rachel?"

"Still asleep, and her granny will be here by lunch-time."

No one was guarding our gate any more and everything outside looked serene and beautiful.

"No telephone calls?"

Angus shook his head. "You'd better get up and help Mum. She's trying to clean up the house," he said.

"Why don't you help?"

"I'm a boy."

"Chauvinist," I yelled, shutting my window.

My back still hurt and all the muscles in my legs were aching from the effort of riding Phantom bareback. After a quick hot shower I struggled into shorts and a shirt then pulled a comb through my hair.

Mum was sweeping the stairs. "Rachel's granny will be here soon, and look at the place," she wailed.

"What does it matter? It looks all right to me, anyway. And at least we aren't spies," I replied.

"But look at the dust."

"Mrs Parkin will be here tomorrow," I reminded her, looking for something to eat in the kitchen. "It's no good keeping a dog to bark and barking yourself."

Munching bread, I telephoned the Carruthers. Alison answered. "Phantom's improving, but homesick. You'll be able to have him soon," she said. I thanked her over and over again, then went outside to see Killarney who was standing in the stable half asleep.

Then Mum called, "Rachel's up. She wants to talk."

I went inside and found her sitting at the kitchen table.

"I hear you saved my life," I said quickly.

"Thank you. Marli isn't dead. We saw her last night."

"I don't believe it." Rachel's hair was uncombed and her tee shirt was on back to front. "You're lying. I heard the shot."

"He was trying to frighten you. I promise you she's all right," said Angus, standing in the doorway.

"How do you know?"

"We went and looked," I answered.

"And Phantom?"

"He's alive too – just," I told her.

"And my parents, my so-called parents?"

"They're still in custody," replied Angus.

"I don't care. I don't care any more. I stood everything until I heard that they were plotting to kidnap you, Jean, and my stepfather said he would shoot Phantom if it was necessary. 'I'll send her father one of his ears,' he said. 'And you won't stop me, Rachel, because if you try to I'll kill Marli.'"

"I would try to forget it," suggested Angus, going to her, putting a hand on her shoulder.

"I shall . . ."

"When did it start and how did you know?" Suddenly I was consumed by curiosity but at the same time I was seeing one of Phantom's ears wrapped in newspaper, pale gold, severed, bloodstained.

"Right from the beginning. They told me to

tell Mrs Parkin I was lonely. They had a whole
folder on you. I had to make friends with you
and get the key and my stepfather promised me
a horse in return," she said. "At first I didn't
think it mattered so much. I didn't think the
plans were that important," said Rachel, beginning to cry.

Angus made mugs of strong coffee for us and
we all sat round the table drinking.

"So it was your father who was the burglar?" Angus said.

"That's right. I told him when you were going to be out. It was that simple," replied
Rachel. "He had your key copied and got in
quite easily. Actually I quite enjoyed it at first,
and then, when I started to like you, I hated it.

Then I got Marli and you were so kind and I wanted to kill myself," she told us, "I kept thinking of ways of doing it, but I wasn't brave enough . . . Then I had to put something in your telephone receiver and that made me feel ill, really ill, and I wanted to die. I could never be a spy, I know that now. I was always in your house and you didn't seem to mind – it was extraordinary."

"But then David Winter isn't your father, is he?" asked Angus gently. "And you had a key to our door, is that what you just said?"

"Yes, my stepfather took an impression and we had one cut, and you didn't seem to notice. You seemed so thick."

"We did notice, but things happened so quickly. I think Dad suspected something all along," I said. Suddenly I felt proud, and afraid at the same time.

"The case will be heard in camera, so not much will come out. Dad won't even be named," said Angus.

"By the way, where is he?" I asked.

"Gone to London on the early train."

"Poor Dad."

"I tried to warn you in lots of ways, but you didn't seem to understand," Rachel said.

"I think we knew deep down inside ourselves," I said.

"And I was so jealous of you, Jean. I still

am," confessed Rachel, putting down her mug.

"Jealous of me? But I'm such a country bumpkin. As Angus once said, if I went to the Ritz I would spill oats on the carpet."

"So what?" asked Rachel.

"People always want to be what they're not," said Angus, going red.

"I don't want to be the way I am. I would like to live in Sparrow Cottage, and have parents who have stayed together, my very own mother and father. I don't care how I look. It's only a disguise. I hate myself really," continued Rachel.

I could think of nothing to say. There was a short silence until Angus said, "Well, I like you the way you are."

I said, "But there's no swimming-pool at Sparrow Cottage."

"Damn swimming-pools. Who wants a swimming-pool?"

"But – " I began again.

"It's all buts, isn't it? But I mean what I say. I hate being Rachel Finbow, though I would hate being Rachel Winter even more. Also, I don't want to live with my grandmother."

I thought: Don't cry, Rachel, please don't cry.

Angus said, "Life goes in stages like the seasons, perhaps you've been going through winter and now it's going to be spring."

Suddenly I saw how lucky we were, with

ponies, parents and Sparrow Cottage and, as I washed up our coffee mugs, I vowed I would never grumble again.

"I know you thought my parents were marvellously hospitable, Angus, but they weren't really. It was all for a purpose. They never give anything away for nothing," said Rachel, going into the garden.

Later Rachel's granny arrived. She was large and kind with two little terriers who yapped incessantly. She kissed Rachel saying, "You look terrible, you poor girl." Mum gave her sherry and they sat drinking while Angus and I went outside and talked to Killarney.

"She'll never get over it; she'll be scarred for life," he said.

"I always suspected she was pretending. She never meant anything she said," I told him, patting Killarney's dapple-grey neck.

"It must have been so terrible for her, so absolutely terrible," exclaimed Angus. "Think of the choice she made to save you."

"And England. After all, her first father died for England defusing a bomb," I told him.

Everything smelled wonderful, of flowers, horses, and mown grass from the house next door. I wanted to lie down and kiss the ground because we were still alive and it was summer.

Then Mum called us in and we all sat round the table in the small, cramped dining-room and feasted on cold meats and salad and potatoes with lashings of mint, followed by apple pie made out of the first of our windfalls, and cream.

I looked Rachel's granny straight in the eye and asked, "What about Marli?"

"I'll make arrangements for her to stay at the stables nearby, but Rachel will have to continue her studies or find a job. There's a good secretarial college in Southampton," she said.

"But is it a good stable?" asked Angus.

"It's approved and has a covered school."

I looked at Rachel, who was staring out of the window as if all the answers were there among the flowers and trees. I wondered whether she would ever be able to adjust to another life.

Angus made coffee which we drank in the garden. Then we piled into the car and went to Hill Farm House. Marli and Maggie were standing in a corner trying to defend themselves from the flies which were everywhere. There was hardly a blade of grass left in the paddock. There were still police in the house, but they let us go up to Rachel's room to put some of her belongings into a suitcase. She was very quiet now and her room was impersonal like a hotel room, rather than one in a private house.

"You can stay with us whenever you like," said Angus, leading the way down the stairs. "I mean it, Rachel – anytime at all . . ."

"After what has happened? You must be mad, Angus," she replied.

"We'll want to hear about Marli," I told her. "Please write."

"You can always telephone," she told us. "But as soon as I can, I shall go abroad. I want to forget this place. My cat died here and Uncle George went out in the woods and died, and my mother and father quarrelled, threatening to tell the authorities what each had done to me and my cat, and Uncle George. Living here has been a nightmare. I never want to come back, never. I hate the place."

The police made way for us. We could hear Mum and Rachel's granny admiring the swimming-pool.

Angus shouted, "Ready. We've finished."

"Marli must be moved soon," I said. "There's no grass left."

"You can find her a home. Send me the money, keep ten per cent for yourself, Jean, you've earned it," Rachel said.

"Don't you want to ride her any more?" asked Angus.

"No, I want all this to be over. I don't want to remember it," she said.

We climbed back into the car in silence. Suddenly everything seemed to have been said. A chapter ended.

"My bike's still at the Devil's Churchyard and my hat is in the woods. I've lost my bridle too," I said as we drove home.

"We'll fetch them tomorrow," promised Mum.

"If they're still there," added Angus.

Rachel seemed like a stranger now. Someone who had appeared like a friend and almost destroyed us and was going, but Angus would always see her as noble. He would keep saying to me, "She saved your life Jean," though it was not true, because Phantom had saved my life and Alison too, when she had taught me how to vault when I was twelve.

How little I knew then that being able to vault on to a horse's back might one day save me from kidnap.

Rachel stayed in her granny's car. I think Angus wanted to kiss her, but she did not give him the chance. Then, just as she left, she opened a window and called out, "Thank you for everything," and we could see that she was crying.

"Do you think her parents really killed George and the cat?" I asked.

"Of course," replied Angus, as though such things happen every day. But who knows – George died of a heart attack.

My story is almost told now. Dad returned later, exhausted. "I'm being given a fortnight's leave, so we can go somewhere nice," he said. "And don't scream, Jean, because you know you can't ride anyway."

"What about Phantom?" I asked.

"Dominic will have him."

"And the police?" asked Angus.

"Everything's been said."

"Not quite. There are a few ends still to be tied up," argued Angus. "What happened to the camera and my cassette-recorder when David Winter raided the place? And who put those awful words above Jean's bed?"

"They were meant to confuse you. To make the police think it was youths robbing the place," Dad answered, sitting down.

"And how did they steal Phantom?" I asked.

"They led him to the end of the lane, then flogged him until they got him into the horse box you must have seen by the ruined buildings, Jean. I guess they kept him in it most of the time," Dad said.

"You seem to know everything," I told him.

"And he had weals all over him so you must be right."

"No, not completely right. I don't think I ever will be. I'm only glad it's over," he said. "I never liked them. I knew they were phoney from the start."

"They don't want Marli," I told him.

"They never did. Rachel won't change now; it's too late," he answered wearily. "What a mess. As for her parents, they will be put away for years."

He made himself some tea, then continued, "But if they had got the plan, a lot of heads would have rolled, not just mine, Jean. They would also have made a fortune, because this new system is unique, the greatest invention since radar. It's so important that it might just alter the whole balance of power. But it has still to be manufactured and that takes time. We need help financially."

Then we heard hoofs in the lane. I rushed out and there was Alison leading Phantom from the saddle of a big bay gelding.

"He was homesick. We've walked here slowly. He's still weak and he won't get well with us. I'm sorry," she said.

I cried, "Thank you," and threw my arms round Phantom's neck, while Mum fetched a cold drink for Alison. He smelled of antiseptic and his mane had been brushed and he was

wearing a leather headcollar with brass buckles. "But he's going to be all right, isn't he?" I asked, looking at his thin sides, at his stomach which was greyhound thin and at the weals which were still there on his shrunken quarters. I was trying not to cry.

"Yes, of course. He's just exhausted and homesick. You can build him up gradually, give him small feeds two or three times a day," she advised.

"With flaked maize and boiled linseed, and boiled barley?" I inquired.

"That's the idea."

"Thank you for bringing him, anyway, and thank you for rescuing me."

"No problem. Old Century needs the exercise, but I must go soon or I'll be caught in the dark. And honestly, Jean, it was Alan who saved you, not us."

"No, not altogether. You saved me, too, because you taught me to vault when I was twelve. Do you remember?"

"Oh, on a little grey mare."

"That's right. I vaulted on to Phantom and fled; otherwise I would have been kidnapped and ransomed and the government would have fallen. So you altered the fate of nations," I finished dramatically.

"What a story. Honestly, Jean, you're going too far," Alison said.

"It was serious, very serious," I answered. "Very hush-hush too."

"To change the subject, what about the chestnut Arab turned out with a donkey. The one at Hill Farm House?" asked Alison, handing me her empty glass.

"Marli?"

"Is that what she's called?"

Putting the glass down I nodded. "And she needs a home," I said. "A good one for ever and ever."

"I know someone who wants one for long-distance riding. She is Arab, isn't she?" asked Alison, pulling up her girth.

"As pure as pure," I answered, and saw that Phantom was grazing the lawn. Later Dad would grumble about the hoofmarks, but now it did not matter, the only thing which mattered was that he was eating. I followed him as he moved from mouthful to mouthful while Alison called, "Can I collect her tomorrow?"

"I don't see why not. I'm in charge. We can meet you at Hill Farm House any time. I'm getting ten per cent and it must be a good home, and the price is not less than three thousand pounds," I called.

"That's fine. I'll meet you about six. Okay?"

"Yes, okay, and we'll get old Maggie moved, too," I shouted. "And thank you again."

I listened to Old Century's hoofs clip-clopping

away before I turned Phantom out and, watching him roll, I knew that the nightmare was finally over. Rachel would go on living it for some time, perhaps for ever, but I would recover and, as I mixed a feed for Phantom, I was filled with a tremendous sense of achievement because, somehow, against all odds, we had survived.